FATE

A New Beginning

KENNIS ANTHONY

Order this book online at www.trafford.com
or email orders@trafford.com

Most Trafford titles are also available at major online book retailers.

Cover Design by Lana Campbell.

Printed in the United States of America.

ISBN: 978-1-4669-8623-7 (sc)
ISBN: 978-1-4669-8625-1 (hc)
ISBN: 978-1-4669-8624-4 (e)

Library of Congress Control Number: 2013906579

Trafford rev. 07/16/2013

 www.trafford.com

North America & international
toll-free: 1 888 232 4444 (USA & Canada)
fax: 812 355 4082

CONTENTS

THE BEGINNING AND THE END

Kneeling down on his backyard basketball court to lace up his old pair of Converse All Stars, Eric Miller reflects that it was a Saturday morning just like this a year ago that he received a call from the Ann Arbor Police of a break-in at his laboratory. He knows his friend Pastor Walls will arrive shortly for their weekly round ball battle, and Eric once again ponders sharing with him some details surrounding his moral dilemma. The police referred to them as thieves, but Eric privately questions the use of that term since he reported to them that nothing was stolen.

The familiar sound of a car horn in his driveway breaks Eric from his capricious thoughts and signals the arrival of Pastor Walls. Eric prides himself on being undefeated on his home court, but the arduous events of the past year have him off his game. The two men are not natural or blood brothers, but one might never know. As members of the same religious persuasion, Pastor Walls is the pastor at Grace of God Church where Eric is his head deacon. Hearing the car door close, Eric walks toward the front of his house to greet his longtime friend. They customarily hug each other without speaking a word.

Then as they retreat to the rear of Eric's home to start their game, Eric warns his friend, "You know I don't lose on my own court, yet you keep coming back for more. Are you a glutton for punishment, or can you really be just that nuts?" Eric reaches into a garbage can where he keeps several basketballs and tosses one toward his friend. "Take it out, Pastor," insists Eric. Pastor Walls steps off the grass in the backyard court at Eric's Ypsilanti, Michigan, home to begin the game. He takes four fast dribbles toward the basket, sending Eric backing up fast on his heels, and then stops and shoots a fifteen-foot jump shot, nothing but net.

"One zip!" shouts Mike, heading back toward the grass. Eric throws the ball back to Mike. Mike makes like he is going to drive again and, just before stepping on the pavement, tosses the ball to a quickly approaching Eric. "Check." Eric catches the ball and approaches his opponent. Slowly giving up the ball, Pastor Walls fakes left, dribbles to his right, but allows Eric to catch up, faking with his head like he is going to attempt another long jump shot but never giving up his dribble. While Eric launches toward his pastor to block what he thought was another jump shot, Pastor Walls drives hard toward the basket for an easy layup. "Two zip," brags Pastor Walls.

"Looks like someone's been practicing!" says Eric. Holding the ball as he walks back to the top of the court where Pastor Walls has retreated and is waiting, Eric continues, "But enough of this." Eric Miller hands the basketball to Pastor Walls. Mike tries the same move that got him the last point, but Eric is ready for it. Eric steals the ball and quickly drives to the basket for an easy layup. "Two-one," shouts Eric. Pastor Walls and Eric, black men in their midforties, neither having biological brothers, have been getting together nearly every Saturday for over ten years. They both love the game as well as each other's companionship.

With the score twenty-nineteen in Pastor Walls's favor, he knows he must win by two points, and the next basket will make him victorious for the first time on Eric's court. Eric Miller guards Pastor Walls closer than the clothes he is wearing. The two near exhaustion, Pastor Walls tries to end the game in the same manner he started it, but Eric is ready. He blocks Pastor Walls's shot and drives toward the basket, tying the game. Eric inbounds the basketball and, in the same manner as his opponent started the game, ends this match with two consecutive fifteen-foot jumpers. The two men shake hands and drag their weary bodies to the adjacent patio deck for a cool drink of water.

"I never came that close," admits Pastor Walls between deep breaths, fatigued from the game. The two sit down without Eric replying to Mike's observation. "To tell you the truth, brother, I have not been practicing, yet I came within two points of winning my first game ever on your court. How did this happen? You okay, man?"

"Yeah, just beat," answers Eric.

"No, I'm the one that got beat!" replies Pastor Walls.

"Don't sell yourself short, Pastor. You were up on your game today."

"Not as much as you seem to be off yours, Eric. What's on your mind? You have not been yourself lately," states Pastor Walls.

Eric grins, rests his hand on his pastor's shoulder, and, chuckling, says, "Very perceptive of you, Dr. Walls, and you are right. You know me probably better than any other person, family or friend." After pausing to sip his water, Eric continues, "I've been struggling with an incident that happened a year ago today. Let me ask you this, Pastor. Would you consider it lying to withhold the truth?"

"Well, Eric," replies Pastor Walls, "as my head deacon, I would hope you could answer that question for yourself. The scripture says all liars are headed to hell. There is no such thing as a white lie or a little lie. A lie is a lie . . . but you know that. What's really on your mind? Does this have anything to do with your abandoning your experiments with that hyperdrive engine you designed, or is it much more serious, like something you have not shared with me?"

Looking Pastor Walls straight in the eye, Eric quickly responds, "What could be so serious, Pastor, that I would hide it from you?"

"One thing that comes to mind immediately is female problems," replies Pastor Walls. "I have counseled many men, and nothing affects us more drastically than those inflected by the opposite sex. In all the years I've known you, you have never once mentioned having seeing a woman. Has there ever been someone special in your life?"

Eric lowers his head, looking down to the ground, and chuckles while convincing Pastor Walls it has nothing to do with a woman. He admits that he is well aware of the adverse effects of not being as forthcoming with facts as he ought. He concurs with the pastor that his quandary does involve his work. He also shares with Pastor Walls that he left because it seems someone was attempting to discredit his work or use the technology he created to unleash unimaginable evil.

Pastor Walls responds by assuring Eric that there is absolutely no way he could predict the future or what would happen if his technology falls into the hands of someone who would pervert it. He needs to proceed with a positive attitude and trust God for the rest. He continues by explaining to Eric that fear and trepidation are by-products of innovation and that he should not be troubled with a nemesis that might not exist. He reminds Eric of what Job said in the scriptures that the thing he feared the most came upon him—that the beginning of one thing brings about the end of another—and how Jesus ushering in a period of grace fulfilled and ended the dispensation of the law. He urges Eric not to let whatever it is that is troubling him destroy him. "I just hope I can squeeze in a win or two before you regain your composure," he adds.

Both men chuckle as they finish drinking their water while walking to the front of Eric's house. "I need to be heading back to Southfield, Eric," declares Pastor Walls. "I want to read over tomorrow's Sunday school lesson again. We good for next Saturday?"

"Same time, same channel," answers Eric.

"Same time, but on my court," insists Pastor Walls, opening the driver's door of his classic 1965 light blue Mustang convertible. He inquires how Eric's 1968 triple white Cadillac Deville convertible has been running, attempting to divert Eric's attention from his issues. Eric opens the garage door and removes the tarp over the Caddy. Pastor Walls, leaving the driver's side door of his car open, approaches the garage. "You had it out since the winter?" he asks.

"Not once," answers Eric, shaking his head.

"Man, this shout needs to be driven, baby! Why don't you break it out tomorrow? After the morning service, we'll take it for a spin. Blow some of that carbon out the engine."

"That'll work," says Eric with a slight smile. "Yeah, that'll work, my brother."

Pastor Walls does not feel comfortable in leaving his friend, aware that Eric never discloses the problem plaguing him. The two shake hands and embrace, as they customarily do, followed by a parting prayer by Pastor Walls. "May the Lord bless thee and keep thee. May the Lord make his face shine upon thee and be gracious unto thee. May the Lord lift up his countenance upon thee and give thee peace. In Jesus's name, amen and amen."

Pastor Walls returns to his vehicle, starts it, and drives away. Eric Miller watches as his friend drives down the long driveway, turns onto the main street, and blows his horn. Eric responds with a wave and watches as the car travels out of sight. Their patio conversation very much fresh in his mind, Eric debates washing his vintage automobile but lacks the motivation to do so and closes the garage door.

Eric enters his home and goes directly into his study. Along with not disclosing the details of his predicament, he thought of something else Pastor Walls alluded to, that being the absence of a significant other in his life. In Eric's study, a bookcase covers one entire wall, extending thirty feet from wall to wall. Five feet in front of the bookcase in the center of the room is his desk. Another five feet in front of his desk is a fireplace. Sitting at his desk, his eyes staring at the flameless fireplace, he realizes there are no pictures on it as in other homes. He swivels his brown leather chair around toward the bookcase and spots an elementary school photo album. Slowly exiting his chair, he retrieves the photo album and finds a fifth-grade class group picture. The entire class was made up of minorities, but he was the only black. Group pictures in that era did not have names on them, and Eric could not remember most them. Of all the memories he had of these classmates, one person stood out as he considers what Pastor Walls said of relationships. He also wonders why he could remember her name.

"Good morning, Mother. Did you sleep well last night?" asks Dr. Erica Myers as she slowly approaches the kitchen table where her seventy-year-old mother is sitting, both women still in their nightgowns.

"At my age, every morning I wake up was a night I slept well," replies the elderly Mrs. Myers. "It has not been easy the last few months with your father not being around, not being in bed next to me. I miss his presence." Mrs. Myers points to a chair across from where she sits, motioning for her only child to have a seat. "Can we talk for a minute?" asks Mrs. Myers in a soft yet serious tone.

Erica, forty-five years old, has spent the past week with her mother in the Bettendorf, Iowa, home she was raised in. It is exactly three months ago that her father died from lung cancer, and Erica has not spent any time with her mother since the funeral. It is now Sunday morning, and Erica knows she has one last day before leaving. She has gone the entire week without telling her mother of her decision to move from St. Paul, Minnesota, to take a new job in Houston, Texas. They have also survived the past week without much talk about her father, whom Erica despises and literally hates since grade school, and she fears the time for this conversation is imminent. Erica pauses and gives her mother a repugnant look before limping to her chair, suspecting what her mother is about to say.

"I know you and Harold . . . uh, your father, did not get along too well, but you'll never know how much he loved you and only wanted . . ."

Erica abruptly interrupts her mother, "How much he loved me? *How much he loved me!* He sure had a heck of a way of showing it. The truth is, Mother, Daddy was always ashamed of me. I was a girl, and I was crippled. I wasn't athletic and never could be the boy or buddy he so desperately desired and passionately preferred. Neither of you could hide that." Her voice cracking, nearly in tears, Erica drops her head and continues, "You couldn't conceal my disability, nor could I. But the truth is, I accepted it. I've had no choice but to accept it. I've gone from two canes to no cane. I've gone from barely walking to an occasional jog in the park. And I've grown from a pathetic little girl to a confident woman with a slight limp. The truth is, Mother, Daddy was ashamed of me, and you never came to my aid. Daddy quenched every chance I had to participate in paraplegic activities with other kids like me, and I believe you concurred with his decisions. It was as if since I couldn't be his pride and joy, I won't be anything else. I can count the number of relationships I've had on one hand, and they have all been within the past few years. I'm close to fifty years old, and my most memorable social moment came in the fifth grade, and Daddy ended that."

"Now hold on, Erica," insists her mother. "If I recall, your father was protecting you from a lot more than you could have realized. You were only in grade school. What did you know about society and life?"

"My point exactly, Mother, my point exactly!" counters Erica. "But let's chalk that one up to racism!"

"Listen, baby, you're all I've got, and frankly I'm not sure how much time is left for me. I don't want our relationship to be like yours and your father's." Wiping the tears that are starting to drop from her eyes, Mrs. Myers continues, "I guess what I was eventually going to say is that I know I sided with your father on many occasions, but he was my husband. I was determined to be a good and supporting wife. I didn't work, so outside of neighbors, Harold was my only friend. Please try to understand that I need you. I need you as my daughter and my friend. I love you so much and am so proud of your accomplishments. I love referring to my daughter as Dr. Myers when I speak of you to friends, and I realize that all you have done has been on your own."

"Oh, Mother, I'm sorry. I should not have lashed out at you like that. The past and Daddy are behind me. You know this is a touchy subject for me. I believe you loved Daddy, and he loved you. But let's not be pretentious, my relationship with Daddy stunk, right up to the end." Erica rises and positions herself behind her mother, wrapping her arms around her. "What do you say we get cleaned up, have some breakfast, and hit the mall? We'll shop till we drop."

"I'd like that," replies Mrs. Myers in a soft tone, drying her tears away. She reaches back and places her hand on top of her daughter's arms still wrapped around her shoulders. "I'd like that very much, Ricky."

Kissing her mother on the head, she says, "It's been a long time since you've called me that. I love you, Mother."

Eric Miller locks the last door of the church as he finishes his duties as a deacon. Heading to Pastor Walls office, he struggles to recall the message from this morning's sermon as he is preoccupied with their conversation that Saturday. Just ahead, Eric notices Pastor Walls's wife, Sandy, leaving her husband's office.

Eric greets her in their common vernacular. "Praise the Lord, First Lady. Will you be joining us for a cruise? I'm buying dinner at Red Lobster!"

"You and Pastor go on, Deacon Miller. I will go ahead and get a table. Someone has to drive our car back home," explains Sandy while holding the door open to the pastor's office. Eric waits as Pastor Walls gets dressed after his shower.

Eric and Pastor Walls take the scenic route to the restaurant some ten miles away. With the top down and barely driving the speed limit, they solicit stares from other motorists and pedestrians. An all-white 1968 Cadillac Deville convertible in pristine condition is not something you see every day. They recollect all the good times they have had in this car, most of which, Eric confesses, his pastor does not know about. Pastor Walls is well aware of the fact that Eric has not fully confided in him. His earnest expectation is that if he continues to keep the dialog free and flowing, Eric might open up about his troubles. While it is a good plan, they arrive at the restaurant without ever coming close to the subject.

Entering the restaurant, the pair asks for and finds the table occupied by Sandy Walls. These three friends enjoy one another's company as well as a good meal. After eating, Eric requests that his confidants continue to remember him in their prayers. Although Pastor Walls and Sandy offer an itchy ear, Eric refuses to share any details outside of the fact that he needs strength for whatever the Lord has in store for him. After Eric pays the tab, they walk to his car. The Wallses pray for Eric before watching him depart.

On the journey to their home, the Wallses discuss their good friend. Pastor Walls shares with his wife the conversation he and Eric had on Saturday, mentioning that Eric believes he might be living a lie. Sandy, in all her spiritual insight, believes the dilemma with Eric is spiritually based. "God has his hand on Deacon Miller, and he really needs our prayers," offers Sandy. "I'm sure it is nothing that a good woman in his life couldn't cure," she adds. Once home, the Wallses spend over an hour in fervent prayer and supplication on Eric's behalf.

Once home, Eric parks his car in the garage and covers it up. He changes from his dress suit to a jogging suit, retreating to his basement gym. He begins a run on his treadmill but cannot jog more than a mile. The spirit of God leads him to immediately get to his knees and pray. Submitting to the will of God, Eric prays for more than an hour. Once done, he showers in the small basement bath outside his gym. Slowly moving to the main level of his home and entering his study, Eric approaches his desk, determined to read his Bible. However, as he pulls out his chair to sit down, he notices the elementary school class photo is still lying on his desk. He can't help but sense God is dealing with him relative to those years, and he asks God to reveal it to him.

Erica and her mother spend the entire day shopping, buying clothes and other tokens of affection for each other, never once hinting at the contentious conversation they had earlier. Yet dislike for her deceased father still weighs heavy on Erica's mind. She wonders, if she had had a religious upbringing, would that have helped her forgive and overcome her animosity toward her father? Throughout the afternoon, she looks at her mother and sees how happy she is that her daughter is spending time with her. Deep down inside, she loves her mother dearly and wants to erase the events of that morning and retract the awful things she had said. An overwhelming sense of guilt could not be shaken for the way she perceived she has been treating her mother. Nevertheless, Erica knows she has to inform her mother of her decision to move but thought it best to wait. Mrs. Myers and Erica finish their outing by visiting a restaurant Erica knows her mother loves. The day seems to pass away quickly.

Erica has been quiet the entire journey home. Upon arriving, they go into the family room and begin sorting through the many packages they have purchased that day. After finishing, each takes their respective items to their rooms. Erica also starts packing. Her mother senses there is something in her daughter's mind and enters into her room. "You mind if I have a seat?" asks Mrs. Myers.

Erica points to the bed. "Of course not, Mother."

"Are we okay, dear?"

"Sure, Mother," replies Erica, not once having looked at her mother.

"So why won't you look at me?" asks Mrs. Myers.

Erica stops packing and sits next to her mother. "I did not want to tell you when I arrived and could not seem to find an opportune occasion, but I will not be going back to St. Paul when I leave here tomorrow. I have accepted a job in Houston. I have leased a house for ninety days. My furniture and my car should already be there. I will spend Monday morning meeting my new bosses and take the remainder of the day to settle in. I'll call you in a few days with my work and home phone numbers, but my cell phone will remain the same." Erica reaches into her purse and withdraws a business card. "Here is my business information."

"The Space Agency?" asks a surprised Mrs. Myers.

"I will be working with the Space Agency as a psychiatrist for astronauts. My interest and work in space navigation was, from what I am told, what separated me from other qualified candidates," explains Erica.

"A new beginning, dear?" asks her mother softly.

"Yes, a new beginning for my career and hopefully for us too, Mother. I want to put an end to our past."

"I love you, Ricky!"

"I know, Mother, and I love you too!"

Mother and daughter embrace, then Erica continues to pack as her mother watches. "Could you hand me that scarf, Mother?" asks Erica, pointing to a scarf draped across a chair in her old room.

"That's my old scarf I got from your grandmother," says Mrs. Myers as she holds it to her face before proudly handing it to her daughter.

"I know that, Mother," replies Eric, knowing her mother delights in her having it.

After watching her daughter meticulously pack, Mrs. Myers falls asleep on the bed. Once finished, Erica moves her luggage and belongings into the living room. Returning to her room, she dutifully positions the covers over her mother, then gently and quietly situates herself in bed next to her. Early the next morning, while her mother is still asleep, Erica showers, dresses, calls for a taxi, writes a note for her mother, kisses her goodbye, and leaves for the airport.

As a black stretch limousine turns off NASA Boulevard onto Saturn Lane, its two occupants prepare to exit. "Welcome to the Space Agency," announces the driver, preparing to hand one of the men his business card receipts. "I trust you will enjoy your stay. Please call the number on the back of this card when you are finished with your business. I'll be just a mile or so away at Wards Park." The limousine driver exits his vehicle and opens the rear driver-side door. One well-dressed, distinguished, older passenger disembarks and squints his eyes as the bright sun beams upon his face. The limo driver proceeds to the rear passenger side of the car, allowing another passenger to exit. A second slightly older and equally well-dressed gentleman likewise frowns at the sky before removing a pair of sunglasses from his shirt pocket to cover his eyes. From the rear of the limousine, they each retrieve a briefcase. The two men walk slowly toward the building. They enter into the lobby at the same slow but steady pace.

"Good morning, uh, Ms. Devereaux," says one man as he reads the name on the receptionist's nameplate. "I'm Professor Hans Mueller, and this is my colleague, Mr. Raymond Richards. We are here to see General Benjamin Westbrook."

Ms. Devereaux, the young statuesque receptionist at the Space Agency, replies with a warm smile and, in a soft yet professional voice, says, "Please sign the register, gentlemen, and I will ring General Westbrook's secretary." As she picks up the telephone, she continues, "What time is your appointment?"

Mr. Richards, now signing the register, answers Ms. Devereaux, "9:00 a.m." He looks at his watch and smiles. "We're a little early."

Ms. Devereaux hands the two men guest badges and points to a waiting area a few yards to her right. "Please have a seat, gentlemen. The general will send for you shortly."

"Thank you, Ms. Devereaux," returns Mr. Richards as he removes his sunglasses. Professor Mueller acknowledges with a nod and ushers his partner to the waiting area.

As the two men take seats across from each other, Raymond Richards whispers to his companion, inquiring if he is certain they are doing the right thing. They have journeyed to Houston from Michigan, the home state of Raymond Richards and his aircraft construction factory, as well as of Hans Mueller and his engineering firm. Two years ago, the two joined forces in an attempt to revolutionize the space industry, and they now seek the Space Agency's assistance.

In a second-floor conference room, General Benjamin Westbrook entertains a small group of men, eager to interrogate the guests that await them. Among them are National Intelligence Agency (NIA) director Walter Kennedy, mission control director David Veil, and William Rodgers, a scientist working on propulsion systems. Sitting at an oval table with proposals in front of them, William Rodgers (known to the group as Bill) directs a question to the general. "Are you seriously considering conjugating with these guys? Have we checked out their credentials? Are you . . ."

"Just calm down a minute, Bill," interrupts the general. "There is more at stake here than just your pride and that of your staff. Walter has information that German scientists working for their government are close to developing a fusion energy source and have consummated a deal with private investors within the former Soviet Republic. We know they can't manufacture a fraction of a gram of antimatter a year, making any containment vessels theoretical and useless at best. Let's not give these guys any reason to take their dog and pony show to the Russians and Germans. While we can't let them know this, we need those men waiting downstairs just as much or more than they need us, that is, unless you have something to share with us today, Bill, that you didn't have yesterday. I can't tell you how important it is we stay ahead of the world in the space race. We can't afford to play catch-up, gentlemen. The agency needs an infusion of new talent and ideas. We need to put behind us the questionable space shuttle era and the mistakes we brought upon ourselves. By partnering with the public and private industry, any and all risk and blame can be diverted away from us. Let's look at this as a beginning of a new era and an end to the old. Now take a few minutes to review the proposals in front of you. I have loaded their visual presentation on the AV system, as requested." Pushing his chair back from the table and standing, the tall, broad-shouldered general continues, "Now if there are no objections, I'll send for our guest."

General Westbrook walks to the back of the plush conference room where a refreshment center takes up the entire wall. He picks up a phone. "Ms. Hayes, will you go down and escort Professor Mueller and Mr. Richards to CR2? When you get here, change out the water and make a fresh pot of coffee." The general returns to his seat and opens his copy of the proposal.

Ms. Hayes gracefully approaches the lobby receptionist. "Liz," she says, referring to Ms. Devereaux, "I feel so much better now that I have been taking the stairs and walking at lunchtime. Fairly soon, I reckon I'll be looking younger and slimmer than you." She glances at the register where their guests have signed in.

"I reckon you better pinch yourself, girl," asserts Ms. Devereaux. The two politely laugh as Elizabeth Devereaux stands and stretches in the manner of a classy model. She then nods in the direction of the lounge where Professor Mueller and Mr. Richards are waiting. "And make sure you're wide awake when you take our guest upstairs, Helen," whispers Liz. "Maybe you can find out what's going on."

Ms. Hayes very professionally approaches the area where the visitors are comfortably sitting. "Good morning, Professor Mueller and Mr. Richards. My name is Helen Hayes, and I will be escorting you to conference room 2, where General Westbrook and his colleagues are waiting."

"Pleased to meet you, Ms. Hayes. I'm Professor Mueller, and this is my colleague Mr. Richards," affirms Professor Mueller as he slightly bows in a gentlemanly fashion.

As Ms. Hayes leads the couple past Ms. Devereaux, she asks, "Would you mind if we take the stairs?" She glances ever so slightly at Liz as she passes.

"Not at all," answers Mr. Richards. "We have been sitting most of the morning and will probably be sitting for a few hours longer. The exercise will be good for us."

Leading them up the stairs, Ms. Hayes turns back and asks, "Is this your first visit to Houston and the Space Agency?"

"Yes, it is," acknowledges Mr. Richards, the closest to Ms. Hayes. "Professor Mueller and I are very excited about being in your beautiful town."

Now that they have reached the top of the stairs, Ms. Hayes holds out her hand in the direction that she wants her guest to follow. "This is CR2, gentlemen." She holds the door open for them to enter. "Across the hallway, you'll find restrooms." The two men enter into the room. General Westbrook stands, as do Walter Kennedy, David Veil, and William Rodgers. "Gentlemen, please welcome Mr. Richards and Professor Mueller."

General Westbrook walks over and extends his hand. "It is a pleasure to meet you, Mr. Richards." He likewise extends his hand to Professor Mueller. "Professor Mueller, it's a pleasure to finally meet you face-to-face. May I introduce Mr. Walter Kennedy of the National Intelligence Agency; Mr. David Veil, mission control director; and Mr. William Rodgers, our lead scientist working on propulsion systems."

"Just call me Bill," says Mr. Rodgers as he and the other men exchange greetings and shake hands. He directs a statement to Professor Mueller. "There's so much I want to ask you concerning your accomplishments." General Westbrook looks at Bill. "Okay, Bill, maybe later," he says as Bill takes his seat.

"Please have a seat, gentlemen, and we'll get started," expresses General Westbrook.

Ms. Hayes, retreating to the back of the conference room, politely interjects, "I'll put on a fresh pot of coffee and get more ice water," as if it were her idea.

"Thank you," replies General Westbrook. Pointing to the remote control for the audio-video equipment, the general continues to speak. "The floor is now yours, Professor. Your presentation has been loaded on the AV system. You have our undivided attention."

Professor Mueller stands and, using the remote control, activates the audio-video system. A slide picturing Professor Mueller and several scientists and engineers standing outside Mueller Engineering is displayed. "My staff and I have designed, developed, and patented a system for harnessing and controlling antimatter," explains the professor in his native German accent. Advancing the slides, Professor Mueller continues, "Here we have an image of an antimatter chamber. Mueller Engineering produces liquid antimatter as well as its containment vessels. Moving to the next slide, members of my staff were instrumental in the development of this energy and have also worked with a former student of mine to design a matter-antimatter engine as seen here. Mr. Richards, and his associates at RNR Industries, designed and built a craft capable of housing this matter-antimatter engine. This prototype ship is why Mr. Richards and I have flown to Houston. We realize that a successful test flight hinges on a relationship with you. We need the sophisticated and long-range telemetry and tracking systems of the Space Agency."

"General, may I?" interrupts Bill Rodgers.

"Go ahead, Bill."

"Professor, this all seems to be too good to be true. We have been trying to manufacture an engine capable of light speeds for the last twenty years. A matter-antimatter engine has been difficult to conceive due to our inability to produce any significant amounts of antimatter. And you speak of this antimatter manufacturing plant as if it were an oil refinery. There are only a couple of facilities in the world that I know of that have the ability to produce antimatter, and their combined yearly yield totals a fraction of a gram. Help me out here."

"Of course, Mr. Rodgers," replies Professor Mueller.

"Please, call me Bill."

"Of course, Bill," Professor Mueller says as he grins and takes his seat. "A former student of mine discovered a method of producing a stable antihydrogen molecule. The discovery nearly cost him his life. He came to me with the results of his experiments, and I was astounded by his theories and his results. I convinced him that if we could harness and contain the power, we could create possibilities that would revolutionize this industry and our world. Mueller Engineering designed a system for containing this energy. He built a laboratory and started producing liquid hydrogen antimatter. The potential yield was so great that I built a facility manufacturing containers that would store this energy. Fear struck our hearts when we realized a signature from the material could be detected. Our containment vessels are constructed in a manner that shields and masks the properties of this energy so that it cannot be detected."

"So let me make sure I've got this right. These shielded containers are able to mask and contain the antimatter?" asks Walter Kennedy. "This would explain why my agency has not detected it. I am concerned about any other devices you have built or thinking of building utilizing antimatter. And how stable is this substance? What is its effect on the environment? And most of all, what kind of threat do you and your colleagues pose to our national security? I do not feel comfortable with the ease and freedom in which you seem to flagrantly delineate the power in your discoveries. I will be investigating you, your company, and your staff."

"I am somewhat appalled by the fact that you want us to just monitor you as you soar around the solar system," adds David Veil. "Did you come here to rub your accomplishments in our faces? If you have progressed this much, surely you have developed a means of tracking and communicating with your own craft. Come on, Professor, we're not idiots, as you seem to arrogantly insinuate."

"Mr. Veil, I sense distrust and envy. I came here to invoke neither emotion," argues Professor Mueller. "Mr. Kennedy, I can truly respect your concerns as well." Thumbing through the pages of his copy of the proposal, Professor Mueller asks everyone to turn to the last page of their documents. "I have listed all projects Mueller Engineering and RNR Industries are developing. We not only welcome any investigation but also invite it. We also would like for you to visit our technology park. If we wanted to hide, we would not have come here. We wanted to share our accomplishments with you, Mr. Veil, not discredit any work you have already done."

Mr. Richards clears his throat a bit and interjects, "You know one thing we had really hoped for outside of a successful and joint maiden voyage into deep space was to have an opportunity to contract with the government to build a few of these crafts for you. We wanted our own nation to be the first to benefit from our remarkable breakthrough. And I'm sorry you feel as you do, Mr. Veil, but frankly we have kicked your butts in developing a craft that your boys can't even conceive."

Tensions in the room could be cut with a knife, and after a few seconds of silence, Mr. Rodgers clears his throat. And just as General Westbrook was about to speak out to keep Bill from making things worse, Bill Rodgers, in a low and apologetic tone, starts to talk. "I will be the first to admit I was a little skeptical about this whole thing. The fact of the matter is I just want to know how you guys got this thing to work. I want to see it. I'm not for reinventing the wheel. Heck, Benjamin, if their stuff flies, appropriate funds from somewhere, and let's buy a couple of 'em."

Mr. Richards turns to Bill and replies, "I don't think we brought a price sheet with us, but you're welcome to take the prototype out for a spin around Mars when we return. Will you turn the projector back on, Professor? Gentlemen, I proudly introduce our yet-to-be-named spacecraft." There is an eerie silence in the room. Using a laser-pointing device, Mr. Richards details the exterior of the saucer-shaped ship. "It has the length and width of a 747 jetliner. The engine runs down the middle of the vessel and is the size of a jetliner's fuselage. The rear of the ship can be identified by the cone-shaped nozzle uniquely designed to blend in with the ship's contour. The hydrogen and antihydrogen fuel and containment systems surround the engine. Carefully mined and cut bdellium stones are at the heart of the containment system and can store enough of the energy to run generators to power the ship's electrical systems. The front of the ship has living quarters for four men, a galley, an infirmary, and, of course, the flight bridge."

"This is amazing, gentlemen!" affirms General Westbrook. "But I must say, I have already agreed this mission is worth our involvement. I'll want David and Bill to verify every aspect of your mission. We will review your flight plan and make any necessary adjustments our protocols demand. We will provide telemetry and tracking for the entire flight. Under my leadership and authority, we will oversee the entire flight. While Bill and David go over your system with a fine-tooth comb, Director Kennedy will make sure nothing, and I mean nothing, out of the ordinary is found in any of your operations—or the only space you'll go into will have bars on it. And most of all, this mission maintains a top-secret status until such time I decide otherwise to go public. Have you decided on a crew?"

"Not conclusively, but we have candidates in mine," answers Professor Mueller.

"Give me that list of candidates so I can screen them. Once I've made the final decision, I will have our doctors examine them, which means they will have to come to Houston. I will also insist that someone from the agency be included in your crew. Now, gentlemen, let's take a quick break and meet back here in, say, fifteen minutes."

Professor Mueller and Mr. Richards take a second to digest what just transpired. Raymond Richards seems to be taken by surprise, given that General Westbrook has made a decision, although favorable, to accept their offer before it is completely presented. He discreetly questions Professor Mueller as to whether he has prior knowledge of this decision, but the professor ignores the inquiry and rises from his position to converse with David Veil. By now, Bill Rodgers is headed toward Raymond Richards. General Westbrook and Walter Kennedy step outside the conference room, into the hallway. "I want these guys checked out thoroughly, Walter. I want to know how many times these genius crushed an ant," demands General Westbrook.

"I'm all on it, General. I'll head back to Washington and give you a complete report in the next day or so." Director Kennedy salutes the general and leaves. General Westbrook regains his composure and reenters the conference room. The six-foot-five two-hundred-fifty-pound four-star general seems pleased to see the dignitaries converse without being coerced. In his mind, he envisions great things.

Veil and Rodgers, recognizing General Westbrook's presence in the room, nonchalantly discontinue their individual conversations to collectively tell the general they truly believe these guys have a breakthrough. "We think this thing will work," explains a rather jubilant Bill Rodgers. This message substantiates the general's thoughts.

"That's what I'm talking about Bill," says General Westbrook. "I think we're all done here. I want those candidates' profiles on my desk no later than tomorrow evening, Professor. I also want a flight plan by close of business on Friday so David Veil can review it."

"We want to thank you for making this possible General Westbrook," acknowledges Professor Mueller as he approaches the general with his outstretched hand.

"I am speechless," adds Mr. Richards. "I only dreamed of accomplishing what has taken place today. Please accept my deepest and sincere appreciation." Mr. Richards extends his hand as well.

General Westbrook shakes their hands and reiterates, "You gentlemen know what I expect and when I expect it. When you are ready to leave, Ms. Hayes will escort you out and give you our direct phone numbers. Good day, gentlemen."

General Westbrook exits the room as only a man of his stature could. Mr. Veil, Professor Mueller, Bill Rodgers, and Raymond Richards exchange correspondence and plan their next steps. As the four men exit the conference room, they are greeted by Ms. Hayes. She verifies their contact information and gives each of them General Westbrook's business cards. She asks them about their transportation needs, and they inform her of the limousine that is close by. She phones the driver from her desk and informs the professor and Mr. Richards that the driver will pick them up in fifteen minutes. Ms. Hayes then escorts the men back to the receptionist's desk, where they turn in their badges.

It's been a pleasure meeting you," says Ms. Hayes. "Enjoy the rest of your day."

After a few minutes, the black limousine arrives. The driver opens each of the rear doors and watches as his passengers exit the building wearing their sun glasses. He addresses them as a professional servant endeavoring to invoke conversation, but neither man responds.

David Veil and Bill Rodgers knock on General Westbrook's open door and without looking at them signals for them to enter by waving his hand. As the flight director, David Veil believes that disqualified him from joining the crew on their maiden voyage. Bill Rodgers believes that makes him the logical candidate, but he is curious why General Westbrook did not make that known, seeing he seems to have this all planned out. General Westbrook told them the doctor that will be interviewing the crew has just been hired and expects her to be in the office today. Her name is Dr. Erica Myers, and she is unaware of the fact she will accompany the crew on this inaugural mission. Sensing the director and the engineer are still standing there, General Westbrook looks up and asks if there is anything else they wish to discuss; otherwise, he would like to return to work.

In a private parking lot behind the Space Agency building, Director Kennedy sits in his car. Within a few seconds after dialing a number on his cell phone, a voice answers in Russian, identifying himself as the Soviet aerospace prime minister. In the same dialect, Director Kennedy informs the Soviet prime minister that he has no reason to believe they should not continue as planned. He assures the prime minister that measures are in place, which will prohibit the success of the American's launch.

Acquaintances, Not Friends

Professor Mueller and Raymond Richards enter the waiting limousine. Neither man has whispered a word to the other since leaving the conference room. The limousine driver senses there is some tension but needs to ask for directions before he takes off. "Where to?" he asks.

"Houston Hobby Airport," answers Professor Mueller.

The seconds of silence turn to minutes before Mr. Richards asks, "You still haven't answered my question, Professor."

"And what question is that?" replies Professor Mueller.

Mr. Richards responds, "I asked you if you had prior knowledge that General Westbrook would accept our proposal. His quick decision did not seem to faze you one bit. Why is it? I get the distinct impression you are withholding information from me."

"What are you trying to insinuate, Raymond?" asks Professor Mueller.

"I insinuate nothing," replies Mr. Richards emphatically. "I've been around you long enough to know from your posture that when General Westbrook agreed to back our project, it was of no surprise to you. You knew, didn't you?"

Staring out the window, not looking at Mr. Richards, a confident professor Mueller replies, "Let's just say I didn't have any doubts."

"Having no doubts and having confidence fueled by insider information can be two different things. Are we not colleagues, are we not partners, and are we not friends?"

"We are colleagues, Raymond, and we are partners in this venture." Turning to look at Mr. Richards, Professor Mueller continues, "We are acquaintances, not friends."

Somewhat shocked by Professor Mueller's statement, Mr. Richards sinks down into his seat. He takes a moment to gather his composure. In the minutes that follow, he reflects back and realizes that the professor's comments have some validity. In the past few years he has known Professor Mueller, they have never been to each other's homes. They have never gone out to dinner or have a drink together. It has been all business.

The stretch limousine arrives at the airport. Professor Mueller hands the driver several large bills. "This should cover your services for the day," suggests the professor.

"Undoubtedly, sir," replies the driver. As customary, the driver exits the vehicle and opens the doors for his passengers. Handing a card to Professor Mueller, the driver expresses, "Please call me the next time you are in Houston, sir, and I will be more than happy to serve you. Have a nice flight." The driver bows his head and returns to his automobile. Just as he opens the door, across the roof of his limo, he spots an attractive woman with a slight limp pulling her baggage. As she walks past Professor Mueller and Mr. Richards, the limo driver suspects she will hail a cab. He can't resist the urge to assist her. He closes the door, circles the front of his car to the passenger side, and sits on the hood. The woman stops near the curb and spots a yellow cab parked behind the limousine. As she walks past the limo and its chauffeur, the driver stands and asks, "Where can I take you, ma'am?"

"Oh, I am going to the taxicab parked behind you, thank you," responds the woman.

"It shall be my pleasure to assist you. I will take you anywhere you want to go for one dollar," insists the driver as he opens the rear door of the automobile. "Let me put your luggage in the trunk."

The woman stops and thinks to herself, *Something's not right. Why would he offer to take me anywhere I wanted to go for just one buck?* "I don't know you," she claims with a gentle smile and innocent voice.

"Do you know any of the drivers in the vehicles behind me? Listen, I have just been blessed to make as much money this morning as I would normally make all day. Please let me return the favor by blessing you in return."

Sensing a sincere spirit, the woman hands the driver her luggage and takes a seat in the rear of his car. The driver closes the door, places the woman's belongings in the trunk, and proudly gets behind the wheel of his car. "Where can I take you, Ms . . . . ?"

"My name is Erica, and I'm going to the Space Agency."

"Well, Erica, believe it or not, my last fare came from the Space Agency. Isn't that a coincidence?"

Professor Mueller and Raymond Richards enter the airport and locate the flight arrival and departure monitors. They check to see which gate their flight back to Detroit will be assigned to. "Gate 19, Professor," says Raymond Richards, pointing to a monitor.

"Lead the way, Raymond!" replies Professor Mueller as he stretches out his hand.

The two men arrive at gate 19. They have over an hour before their scheduled flight leaves, and there is no attendant at the gate. "How about that long-overdue drink, Raymond?" asks Professor Mueller as he looks around to see which direction the nearest bar is in. "I believe there's a restaurant just past gate 22. A bite to eat might also be a good idea."

"Lead the way, Professor," suggests Raymond Richards.

Professor Mueller grins at Raymond Richards as they slowly walk down the corridor and enter the restaurant. A sign displays the phrase "Please Wait to Be Seated."

A hostess arrives holding up two fingers. "A table or the bar today?" she asks as she starts into the restaurant.

Professor Mueller replies, "A booth would be nice if you have one available."

"Right this way, gentlemen. Is this okay?" she asks.

"This is perfect," replies the professor as they sit down.

"Can I get you something to start off with?" inquires the hostess, placing a menu in front of each of them.

"I'll have a light beer," requests Professor Mueller.

"Make that two," adds Raymond Richards.

"Your waitress for today is Denise. She will be right with you." Both men say thanks, and the hostess departs.

"It has been a long time since I had a juicy burger," notes Raymond. "That and a beer or two should hit the spot."

Without reading the menu any further, Professor Mueller decides that sounds good to him as well. "When Denise gets here, order the same for me too. I'm going to the little boy's room." Professor Mueller scoots out of the booth and heads for the restrooms.

When Professor Mueller returns, a cold beer is waiting for him. Just a few minutes later, their food arrives and Denise offers to bring them another beer when they finish the ones they have. Professor Mueller and Raymond Richards enjoy their food and compliment their waitress. They have another beer after finishing their burgers. Raymond insists on picking up the tab, and Professor Mueller allows it. They leave a generous gratuity before departing the restaurant.

Arriving back at gate 19, a flight attendant has informed the passengers that they will begin boarding the plane in just a few moments. The flight crew is on board and will signal the attendant when ready. Professor Mueller and Raymond Richards check in.

"You have some idea of who you'd like for our maiden voyage, Professor?" inquires Mr. Richards as he attempts to put the statement Professor Mueller made about their not being friends behind him, but he finds it difficult to do so.

"Yes, I do, Raymond. Let's get seated, and we can go over them together. I'd like to get your opinion. I'm sure you have some ideas."

"Professor, did you have prior knowledge our proposal would be accepted? How much do you know?"

"I know when to speak and when not to, Raymond. Please don't speak to me again of this matter," requests Professor Mueller politely.

The flight attendant calls for all first class passengers to board. Raymond Richards nods his head at Professor Mueller, accepting his nonverbal request to proceed ahead of him, and stands, extending his hand in the direction of the Jetway. Both men board the plane, find their seats, secure their briefcases, and prepare for takeoff. Neither man speaks to the other during the entire flight.

The limousine driver announces the arrival at the Space Agency. "Would you like me to wait for you?"

"That won't be necessary," replies Erica. "How much do I owe you?"

"As I told you, one dollar," smiles the driver as he exits the vehicle and opens the trunk to retrieve her bags. Circling to the passenger's side rear door, he opens it and extends his hand. "I sincerely hope you will allow me to be at your service the next time you require transportation. Here is my card." Erica hands him a dollar and takes his card. The driver assists her with her bags, taking them into the building as she walks beside him. "Have a blessed day, Erica."

Erica approaches the receptionist desk and signs the register. The receptionist notices Erica's name and picks up the phone. She quietly dials an extension and holds up a finger motioning for Erica to wait. After softly speaking to someone on the other end of the line, the receptionist hangs up the phone. She reaches for a badge.

"Welcome to the Space Agency, Dr. Myers. This is a temporary badge. General Westbrook has been expecting you. I have contacted General Westbrook's secretary, Helen Hayes, who will come down and escort you upstairs. She will see to it you get through

HR and orientation where you will receive your permanent badge. Please have a seat in the waiting area. Ms. Hayes will be with you directly."

Observing the nameplate on the receptionist's desk, Dr. Myers responds, "Thank you very much, Ms. Devereaux." Erica takes a seat in the waiting area. Her first impressions of her new employer are majestic. As she waits, she reflects on her decision to launch a new career in a new town. Her prompt and rather instantaneous acceptance into the Space Agency has Erica curious as to what her first assignment will entail. Erica knows she has diverse talents that could enable her to exceed where her contemporaries might fall short. She is confident her unique combination of abilities is the reason she is sitting in the Space Agency's lobby, moments away from meeting one of the top-ranked military officials associated with space exploration. Erica attempts to relax, but her anxieties overwhelm her desire to unwind. Nevertheless, Dr. Erica Myers is thankful and appreciative of the opportunity that lies before her. Therefore, she sits patiently.

David Veil and Bill Rodgers have reviewed all the material left by Professor Mueller and Mr. Richards and wait in CR2 for General Westbrook's scheduled briefing. For the exception of inquiring about the crew, they have not left the conference room where the hyperspace spacecraft was unveiled that morning. They still wrestle with the enormous possibilities this technology could produce as well as the disappointments and setbacks if it fails. They suspect General Westbrook's rapid decision to proceed with this experiment was coerced and wait for the opportunity this briefing will present to confront him. Seconds later, General Westbrook enters the conference room.

"Bill, David, sorry I'm getting back to you just now," explains General Westbrook in his usual confident and demanding tone. Without hesitation, he continues, "Well, let's hear it, gentlemen. I'm anxious to hear what you have to say." Neither David Veil nor Bill Rodgers speaks a word in response. Rather, they stare intensely at the general. "Okay, guys, what's with the insidious behavior?" asks the general.

Bill Rodgers and David Veil eye each other as to who will be the first to repudiate General Westbrook's unsubstantiated actions. After a moment of silence, Bill Rodgers begins with an indictment. "General, I, we believe you have information regarding this proposed mission that you have not shared with us. When you presented this proposal to us last week, we did not think you were serious; but when these guys showed up this morning, you had already made up your mind. I figured they were just a couple of loonies expecting the government to finance their dreams, but after reviewing their work, I realized my dreams could become reality. Then it hit me, General, you knew everything. You and your friend from the NIA . . ."

"That's enough, Bill," interrupts a visibly angry General Westbrook. "As long as I am in charge of this program, I will do everything in my power to make it successful and keep this country strong. I'll share information with you on a need-to-know basis. If I don't think you need to know, I won't share it. I don't report to you; you report to me. I appreciate your concern, but don't dare question my rationing of knowledge." Then in a sarcastic and less passionate posture, he continues, "How do you think I got to be a general? Oh, yeah, another thing, Walter Kennedy is an acquaintance, not a friend. Now boys, all we have to do is monitor this flight. The only thing I want to know from you is will this ship fly? If so, come up with a plan for tracking it."

Somewhat embarrassed by his statements, Bill Rodgers apologizes for his remarks. He highlights a few minor issues in need of investigation but assures the general they will have a flight plan on his desk by the end of the week. David Veil asks General Westbrook if the team doctor has arrived or was that also on a need-to-know basis. General Westbrook gives David Veil that look like you're pushing it then informs him that their new team psychiatrist, Dr. Myers, has arrived. Her first full day of work will be Tuesday morning. After the general leaves, David turns to Bill and in a joking manner tells his colleague that he knows exactly how to track the spacecraft, but the general didn't need to know it. "And they say scientist don't have a sense of humor!"

General Westbrook walks into his office and, standing beside his desk, activates his intercom. "Helen, will you escort Dr. Myers to my office? Also, contact the personnel department and verify if her security clearance and badge access have been cleared."

"My pleasure, General," Ms. Hayes enthusiastically replies. She then dials a series of numbers putting her in contact with the employee personnel department. Seconds later, she hangs up and escorts Dr. Myers from the lobby.

Officially a Space Agency employee, Dr. Erica Myers now sits in her boss's office preparing for her first assignment. General

Westbrook explains the facilities and locations to her, where her security clearance will and won't allow her to go, and the agency policies. She will be working with Flight Director David Veil and Engineer Bill Rodgers. He suggests she secures her credentials then take the remainder of the day to get settled in her home. She can meet her team and report to work tomorrow morning. He informs Dr. Myers that her first assignment will be to evaluate candidates for extended missions into deep space. General Westbrook informs her that her interest in space navigation gave her an exceptional advantage over other equally qualified candidates. After inquiring as to why this edge could be considered an advantage, General Westbrook assures her it will become obvious in the not to distance future.

Dr. Myers takes a cab to her new home. She drops her baggage just inside the door and takes a deep breath seeing her furniture has arrived, but she is uncertain as to exactly how she will arrange it. She sits down in her living room and browses around. Uncomfortable, she moves to an empty room that will eventually be her study. Standing there for a few seconds, she goes into the kitchen. Seconds later, it occurs to Erica that she is in need of groceries. She opens empty cabinets as if to find some hidden treasure. Standing at the kitchen sink, Erica thinks it best to buy a few items but has no idea where the closest market is located. Walking past the refrigerator, she instinctively opens its door. Her heart beats rapidly wondering how a bottle of champagne has found its way into the empty icebox. Slowly removing it, she notices a small note attached to it. It is a welcoming present from the realtor who sold her the house. She embraces the bottle, closes the refrigerator door, and returns to a chair in her living room. She reflects how it was the realtor who opened the house for the movers to deliver her belongings. Popping the cork, Dr. Myers doesn't even consider searching for a glass. Immediately, she turns the bottle up and takes a slow and short yet deliberate taste. Allowing the beverage to linger in her mouth for a second, she swirls it around before swallowing, literally envisioning the cool liquid flowing through her system to her stomach. Next, she quickly gulps three to four mouthfuls before removing the bottle from her lips. The effervescent begins to take its numbing effect. Dr. Myers's thoughts suddenly move to her mother. Not having a landline installed yet in her new home, she stands to get her cell phone, and the alcohol intoxicates her further. It's been over a year since she has had a drink. Having retrieved her cell phone from her purse and almost in tears, she returns to her chair. Thirty minutes past before she dials her mother. The telephone rings three times, and the answering machine starts. Erica leaves her mother a brief message informing her she arrived in Houston safely and her first day at work went well. She ends the phone call relieved not having to talk to her mother directly. Another few sips polish off the champagne. Thoughts rapidly race through her mind. She is a foreigner all alone in a big town. She has a new career, a new home, and a new mortgage. What is happening to her, she thinks. The aphrodisiac has put Erica Myers in somber remembrance of her recent visit with her mother. It has seduced her so much that she falls asleep in her chair.

The airplane carrying Professor Mueller and Raymond Richards has landed in Detroit. The men have no luggage and proceed directly to the shuttle bus area. As they stroll through the concourse, they comment on the beautiful new facility. Passing one of the stores selling area memorabilia, Mr. Richards remembers he promised his wife, Pat, a souvenir from Houston. "Do you think I should return to Houston and get that shirt I promised my wife, Professor?" asks Raymond Richards.

"You never know, you might be getting back to Houston sooner than you think," replies Professor Mueller.

"Is there something else I should know?" insinuates Raymond Richards.

"Hold on now, Raymond. That was just a joke. What do I know? I'm single. I can afford to say such things. I have no one to make promises to."

Professor Mueller chuckles, but Mr. Richards's just smiles. By now, they have made their way outside and have begun to look for the shuttle that will take them to short-term parking, where Professor Mueller's automobile is parked. Waiting only a few moments, a yellow van arrives and picks them up. They are the only passengers.

"Section 2A," instructs the professor to the shuttle driver as they begin their short journey. Minutes later, the driver shouts out, "Where in 2A?"

"The black Mercedes on the left please," answers the professor as he prepares to give the driver five dollars.

Professor Mueller unlocks the car with his remote, and both men take their seats. As they drive to the attendant's booth to pay their bill, Professor Mueller looks at Raymond Richards and asks him if it would be okay if they went to Raymond's office to discuss their list of candidates. Raymond Richards, while wondering why his colleague has just now decided to discuss this matter, responds favorably to the offer. He wonders whether Professor Mueller is aware that he has a wife to go home to, but he does not want to stir the professor's emotions. As with the journey from Houston, the trip to Ann Arbor is hauntingly silent.

The workday has ended when Professor Mueller and Raymond Richards arrive at RNR Industries. Located just north of downtown Ann Arbor and the university, the facility is well hidden among five hundred acres of nature. Security is very tight at Raymond Richards's factory, presently housing the spacecraft that will soon make its maiden voyage into outer space. Turning onto a paved road lined with pine trees, Professor Mueller drives a quarter mile to a well-designed and maintained guardhouse. A security guard verifies Professor Mueller's identity and opens the electronic gate. From the guardhouse, the road extends another fifty yards before making a ninety-degree turn into a massive assortment of well-landscaped trees and shrubbery. Just beyond the trees, the road splits into two directions. The left branch leads to two buildings divided by a parking lot. One of the structures is a huge aircraft hangar, and the other is a massive factory complex. The right branch of the road leads to a two-story black glass office building. This time of the evening, the surrounding scenery beautifully reflects off the structure. The few outsiders who visit the grounds always pause before continuing on to the front of the building's parking lot. This view momentarily overcomes Professor Mueller before he drives to the front of the office building's parking lot.

"This building always does something to me, Raymond. What on earth ever provoked you to come up with such a stunning design," comments Professor Mueller.

Mr. Richards humbly responds, "Of all the objects of beauty I have created or been a part of"—he pauses as he looks toward the aircraft hangar—"the flying saucer in that hangar delivers an incurable stimulus."

"Isn't that the truth, Raymond? Let's head in and discuss our crew."

The two entrepreneurs exit Professor Mueller's car and retrieve their briefcases from the trunk. An entrance code is entered into the security system by Raymond Richards. A small audible beep indicates the door may now be opened. The two men eventually enter Raymond Richards's executive office suite. Raymond notices a red light flashing on his desk phone. He asks Professor Mueller to have a seat as he clears his voice mail messages. Professor Mueller offers to wait in an adjacent conference room for his colleague, but Raymond Richards insists it will only take a minute and, pleading with Professor Mueller to be seated, extends his hand in the direction of a small conference table in the middle of the room. He simultaneously dials a series of numbers accessing his messages. Professor Mueller cannot help but to notice an uneasy demeanor associated with Raymond Richards as he jots down some figures on a scratch pad. In a tone regulated by an elevated heartbeat, Raymond Richards indicates he is ready to proceed. He removes the top sheet from the scratch pad and takes a seat opposite Professor Mueller.

"A friend of yours, Raymond?" asks Professor Mueller.

"How did you put it, Professor, an acquaintance, not necessarily a friend? Now how about we knock out this list? The ship was designed for a maximum of four people. I think we should plan on filling three seats as General Westbrook indicated the Space Agency will no doubt want to include a doctor."

"Well, Raymond, I believe General Westbrook will want to monitor our progress from within. While the government might not publicly support us, they will want to remain very close to our work." After pausing for a moment, Professor Mueller continues, "A standard crew consists of a pilot, a copilot, a navigator, and an engineer."

"George Lee is the best pilot I have. He designed the saucer and knows every millimeter of the ship. Chuck Johnson is supposed to be an excellent navigator. Having joined us just a couple of months ago, his experience in astronomy could prove to be useful," explains Raymond Richards. "While RNR Industries built the saucer, its engine design came from Eric Miller, one of your former students. His expertise during construction, especially relative to the engines, would make him the logical choice as the mission engineer. Don't you agree, Professor?"

Taking a deep breath, moving away from the table, and running his hands over his mostly bald head, Professor Mueller quietly states, "All your suggestions are logical, but persuading Eric Miller might take some doing."

"Why, may I ask, did he just walk away from this project, Professor? I'm not trying to be nosey, but I believe we were both counting on him seeing this thing through. His knowledge is irreplaceable."

Again taking a deep breath, Professor Mueller confesses, "This is my problem, Raymond. You are correct; there is really no other choice for mission engineer than Mr. Miller. It is imperative we have his expertise on this mission to ensure its success. I have been neglecting to confront him, but I've run out of time. I will see to it he joins this crew. I agree with your selection of George, but I don't really know Chuck. If you think he is solid, I'll buy it. Let's hold off on selecting a fourth crew member. I don't want to have to bump someone knowing General Westbrook wants to insert his own candidate." Squirming in his chair, Professor Mueller uncharacteristically prepares to depart without any further conversation. He rises out of his chair and apologizes to Raymond for needing to be excused. He leaves the room and heads down the stairs, with Raymond at his side. A few feet from the front door, he realizes he has left his briefcase in Raymond's office. Refusing Raymond's offer to retrieve it for him, Professor Mueller returns to the plush office, leaving Mr. Richards in the lobby of his building. Finding his leather brief case, he also finds the scratch pad that Raymond used to write on while listening to his voice message. He tears off the top sheet and lightly colors over the paper using a pencil from his case to reveal a phone number. He places the paper and pencil in his brief case and returns to the lobby. The two men shake hands and agree to meet again tomorrow.

Both men live only minutes away yet arrive to very different homes. Normally, Pat and Raymond Richards eat dinner together, but not knowing when her husband would be home, Pat Richards has eaten and put dinner away. Raymond Richards enters his home and greets his wife of over twenty-five years with his usual hug and kiss. However, tonight he holds her for an exceptionally longer interval. While they embrace, Pat Richards whispers to her husband that his loving gesture will not compensate for his forgetting to purchase her souvenir shirt. Raymond smiles and accepts the fact that his wife knows him all too well. He is not angry for her putting dinner away, and she does not harass him for forgetting a souvenir. While holding hands, they walk into their den and prepare to share each other's day. Pat Richards is excited about the possibilities space travel will bring, possibly discovering new forms of life. She anticipates good news relative to her husband's trip.

"So tell me all about your trip," requests Pat Richards with a girlish innocence.

"I'm not really sure how this day went," replies a visibly disturbed Raymond. "I need some time to put the events of today into some perspective, dear."

"We've always been open with each other, Raymond. I'm not just some acquaintance. I'm you wife and your friend. What's going on?"

Sitting next to his wife, Raymond explains, "I might have made a mistake. I am entering into a venture with someone I know little about. My colleague is an acquaintance, and by his own admittance, we are not friends. I believe he has me under suspension, and I believe he knows something I don't."

"So when did this all start?" asks a puzzled Pat Richards.

"Somehow, dear, the NIA got wind of what we are doing. It was them that sent Chuck Johnson to me. He was showcased as some super pilot who would see to it our mission was a success. But I swear he seems more like a washed up drunk, and I don't trust him. I was told his presence was top secret, but I truly believe Professor Mueller suspects something, even me. He seemed upset when I inquired if he had inside information or insight as to why the Space Agency without question is backing us. Tonight, there was a message on my answering machine from the NIA."

As Pat snuggles closer to her husband, she offers him some comfort. "Don't you think you might be jumping to conclusions? You're just a little nervous. If I didn't know any better, I'd think you were one of the persons planning on going into outer space. Why don't you just explain this all to Professor Mueller? After all, he's your partner! You owe him that much. Professor Mueller is a reasonable and intelligent man. He will listen to you. When you first began building this ship, I thought it was wrong, but now I'm rather excited." Standing and extending her hand toward her husband, she continues, "I know what will take your mind off your troubles."

In a very different setting, Professor Mueller contemplates how he will approach Eric Miller. After an hour or so of meditating in his study, Professor Mueller decides if it is to be done, it must be tonight. He is leveraging the strength of their friendship as a basis for having this conversation. He recalls the last time they spoke. It was nearly three months ago in the saucer's hangar. Eric left without saying any more than "something wasn't right." It's that statement that disturbs Professor Mueller the most. How it was that the very person who invented, designed, and assisted in the manufacturing of the hyperspace engine and the ship's aerodynamics could walk away from what was basically his project from its conception. What Eric

Miller perceived wasn't right ate Professor Hans Mueller like a cancer. So in a non-premeditated moment, he picks up the phone at his desk and dials Eric's number. After a couple of rings, Professor Mueller prepares to address Eric Miller's answering machine but hangs up the phone suddenly for lack of a rehearsed message. He reaches for his desk pen when suddenly an unexpected ring from the phone causes him to jump and to suddenly retract his outstretched arm. After the second ring, the professor wishes he has caller ID. By the third ring, his heart rate has stabilized, and he picks up the telephone handset. His greeting sounds more like the color of a banana than hello.

"Professor Mueller, this is Eric Miller. My phone just rang but I did not have time to get it. I noticed your number was on the display. Did you mistakenly dial my number?"

"No . . . no, Eric Miller. It . . . it was no error. I indeed dialed your number. I hope I have not bothered you?" asks Professor Mueller.

"No bother at all, Professor Mueller," claims Eric. "I should have called you weeks ago, but I could not find the words to express the feelings I've been having. I would rather speak to you in person, Professor. I owe you that much. Would tonight be good for you?"

Extremely relieved by the unexpected course of the conversation, Professor Mueller replies, "I will be home all evening, but there is something I must do, and I could use your assistance. Please do not hang up from this call. Meet me in fifteen minutes at that restaurant on Michigan and US23. I'll explain everything then. Remember, fifteen minutes, and don't hang up the phone."

A very confused Eric Miller follows his mentor's directions. He sets the telephone handset on his desk where he received the call, grabs his keys, and heads toward his garage. After entering his car but before starting it, he bows his head and says a silent prayer, "Lord God and Father of our Lord and Savior Jesus Christ, I thank you. I thank you this evening for saving me and for the opportunity to confront my fears. I ask you tonight to lead me and guide me through the Holy Spirit that resides within me. In Jesus's name I pray, amen and amen." Eric starts his vehicle and heads for the rendezvous point. Likewise, Professor Mueller leaves his home with the phone still off the hook. He admires the way fate has presented the opportunity to discuss the details of the mission as well as get to know what is on Eric Miller's mind.

Fifteen minutes later, Professor Mueller drives up and parks his car next to a waiting Eric Miller. Professor Mueller drops his driver side window as does Eric. "Please get in with me, Eric," insists Professor Mueller. Upon entering Professor Mueller's car, the professor continues, "I'm glad you didn't go into the restaurant to wait for me. It's very good to see you, Eric." Eric returns the sentiment and fastens his seat belt. Not sure what's going on with his mentor, he cautiously assumes an understudies posture. Professor Mueller puts his vehicle in gear and proceeds toward the expressway. "I know you have some questions, Eric, as do I. You might not be aware of the fact that we have completed the last few details on the ship. Raymond Richards and I returned this afternoon from Houston, where we have solicited the Space Agency's assistance in tracking our spacecraft on what we hope will soon be its maiden voyage. Early this evening, Raymond Richards and I drafted a crew list, which included you. We also decided I would be the one to approach you. Your knowledge of the ship is invaluable to the mission's success, and your concerns are invaluable to me. Listen, my young friend. I fear something is terribly wrong and need answers to questions I don't have. I am also interested in why you suddenly left the program and if your concerns and my fears are related."

Looking sharply at Professor Mueller, Eric insists, "I was your student, you are my mentor, we are acquaintances, and I hope we're friends. Friends honor and trust each other. Please tell me I can trust you, Professor."

"I don't think you would be here, Eric Miller, if you did not trust me," replies Professor Mueller.

TRAVELING HERE AND THERE

" **S** o then, now that we trust each other . . . ," states Professor Mueller.

But then Eric interrupts, "Where are we going Professor? Why are we speeding down US23 like bats out of hell?"

"I can't tell you all the details because I don't know them. I'm trying to put things together even as I drive. Right now, I'm going to make a phone call."

"And you have to speed down the freeway to do so? Here, use my cell phone!"

"Please, Eric, my young friend, tell me why you left the program?"

Silence enters the vehicle as Eric stares out his passenger's side window into the dark. Nearly a minute elapses before he decides to answer Professor Mueller's question. "Professor, the only reason I'm here tonight is that I must get this off my chest, and I don't know exactly why, but I do trust you. I need you to trust me and believe everything I'm about to tell you." Turning and looking directly at Professor Mueller, Eric continues, "This must stay between us, Professor. You have got to promise me that!"

"Eric, just today did I start feeling that there could be something very wrong going on here, but I can't prove anything.

What you know could assist me in putting this all together, or it could mean nothing at all. Right now, for whatever our reasons, we need each other. Whether you tell me what's going on with you or not, this mission needs you. Your fate, the fate of this technology, and that of the planet for that matter are all linked together."

"All right, Professor. You know, of all the things that have occupied my mind the past few months, I really believe my destiny is linked to this project." Pausing for a few seconds, Eric resumes, "It all started a year ago when someone broke into my lab. I thought nothing of it at first because it did not appear as if anything was stolen. I noticed the blueprint cabinet had been tampered with and figured the thieves were just rumbling through my files looking for something of value. I had just finished assembling the fuel injectors. The massive antimatter fuel injectors are essential to the hyperdrive system and must be manufactured to exact specifications. Various manufactures from all across our nation assisted in fabricating the delicate components of these injectors. Because of the size of the injectors, I kept them in a separate storage area in the lab. A quick survey the night of the break-in revealed they were still there, all eight of them. I therefore reported nothing missing to the police. Nine months later as we were building the ship, I noticed something odd when assembling the fuel injectors. There were these unusual pressmarks on the casing covering the bdellium crystals, pressmarks not found on the ones I manufactured. Upon closer examination of other engine components, I found similar irregularities. I took some of the strange components to my lab and found them to have major defects and manufacturing flaws. They were replicas and flawed replicas at that. In the days that followed, I went through every engine component and replaced the inferior ones.

"Hold on, Mr. Miller," interrupts Professor Mueller. "I have to stop here."

Professor Mueller exits the expressway and turns onto a poorly lighted side street. Having just crossed the Ohio border, he turns onto a rural road. Driving slightly less than the posted speed limit, Professor Mueller acts as if he is looking for something in particular. Eric maintains his silence but wants desperately to offer some assistance. Suddenly, Professor Mueller makes a sharp U-turn and heads back in the direction they just came. Again, the professor makes a violent turn, this time onto a dark side street and into the parking lot of an abandoned building. Now Eric is praying that this is not his last trip with his mentor. He silently prays that Professor Mueller has not lost control of his faculties. He silently prays that the local authorities do not arrest them for doing that which he has no idea of what they are doing. Professor Mueller turns off the headlights and exits the vehicle without saying a word. He looks around suspiciously as he closes the car door. Eric watches as the professor enters a dark phone booth. He has now become more frightened than puzzled. His next thought takes him back to Professor Mueller asking him to leave his phone off the hook, followed immediately by the recurring thought that his being here with the professor will lead to some truths. He now recalls the professor stating he had to make a phone call. He sees a light come on in the booth just long enough for Professor Mueller to dial a series of numbers from a piece of paper retrieved from his vest pocket. After dialing the number, he opens the phone booth door extinguishing the light. Eric believes Professor Mueller deliberately turns his back so he cannot determine his actions. Professor Mueller swiftly hangs up the phone and strolls back to his vehicle, constantly looking around. He enters the vehicle and pulls off slowly. Professor Mueller turns on his headlights and maintains the posted speed limit. He looks at Eric and states, "I know this might seem odd, my young friend, but believe me I'll explain everything. So now, finish telling me about those counterfeit injectors."

Pleased that the professor has been listening to him and feeling he has nothing to lose, Eric continues describing the events that led to his departure. "What the heck, Professor," replies Eric as his heartbeat returns to normal. "I worked late nights and early morning hours on the ship replacing parts so that no one would suspect what I had discovered. I ran a series of simulations to verify the quality of my components. Once the replacement of the engine components was completed, I made copies of blueprints kept in the hangar at RNR Industries. They turned out to be forged copies when compared to my originals. I traced the counterfeit parts to a company in Germany that was being financed by Russians. All of the blueprints had our signatures on them, Professor; however, microscopic examination revealed that a stamp had been used to sign the documents. I knew this wasn't right because we hand signed our signatures on all our work. I also initialed blueprint revisions, and that signature stamp was missing from key drawings. I should have come to you with these findings, Professor. But I did not know how involved you were in this elaborate conspiracy. Feeling confident that the structural integrity of the spacecraft had not been compromised and all substandard engine components have been replaced, I left the project."

A bewildered Professor Mueller takes a deep breath and runs his hand through what little white hair he has left. After nearly a minute of making various frowns and jesters of anger, he speaks, "Schufts!"

"I'm not sure what you just said, Professor, but I'm sure it wasn't Merry Christmas," expresses a somewhat calmer Eric, sarcastically.

"I'm sorry, Eric, my young friend. I believe what you say is true. Believe me when I tell you I had absolutely nothing to do with this. But this could only mean one thing."

Both men look at each other and respond in unison, "Another ship . . ."

"Yes, my young friend, another ship of some sort. Let me explain it from my viewpoint. You see, I did not suspect anything until late this afternoon. Raymond Richards asked me shortly after our meeting with General Westbrook, the Space Agency's top government official, if I had insider information, which he based on General Westbrook's sudden acceptance of our proposal. At the time, that alone didn't bother me, but he became obsessed with it, to the point I asked him not to bother me anymore about it. After Mr. Richards and I left Houston this morning, we knew we needed to assemble a crew. We met in Raymond's office to review the candidates. Before we got started, Raymond ran through his voice mail messages and seemed to get nervous at one call. He wrote down a number on a piece of paper. I'm not sure what came over me, but I think this is the point that I started to suspect something might be wrong. I managed to get a copy of the number, which I dialed a few minutes ago. A voice recording of Walter Kennedy at the NIA answered the phone. I quickly hung up. So I ask you, what's the NIA doing calling Raymond Richards's office?"

"Who the heck is Walter Kennedy?" asks Eric. "And what does the NIA have to do with another ship?"

"I am also wondering about what Richards knows," says Professor Mueller. "Not long after you left the program, George Lee determined that the ship was completed and would soon be ready for some interplanetary test flights. Raymond and I put together a proposal and submitted it to the Space Agency. Having no means to track the vessel, we thought the Space Agency's telemetry systems were the only way to accomplish this. General Westbrook heads this division. Along with some other Space Agency personnel at the meeting was Walter Kennedy, director of the National Intelligence Agency."

"And the Space Agency has agreed to this?" asks Eric.

"Yes, my young friend, and without hesitation."

"That is so not like our government, Professor."

"Not if they know, or suspect as we do, that there exists another vessel. In which case, our government would do anything it could to have their own ship and be the first to launch it."

"Oh, God . . . this is incredible! Do you think someone inside of Raymond Richards's organization, possible Raymond himself, broke into my lab and has given the Germans and Soviets our plans? Do you think someone inside RNR Industries had something to do with the counterfeit manufacturing of my engine components? So what do we do next, Professor?"

"We go back to our homes and hang up our phones. I did this so that no one would suspect me of making the call should it be traced. For all practical purposes, we had this conversation in our respective homes. With your permission, I will notify Raymond Richards tomorrow that I have convinced you to rejoin our team."

"I take it you will keep our suspicions between us?"

"Oh absolutely, or else I would be admitting to stealing confidential information from his office. I don't believe he suspects me of withholding information, but he might think I'm on to him, as well as General Westbrook," replies Professor Mueller. "At some time, I will have to confront him, but not now. I need to make sure he is not the mole and the intruder is exposed. I need to make sure the mission is not in jeopardy. We will contact General Westbrook and give him the crew assignments. His NIA contact, Walter Kennedy, will no doubt want to screen you all. That might mean taking a trip to Houston. Nevertheless, we must go about our duties, business as usual."

"I've always wanted to go to Houston. Just curious, Professor, who are the other crew members, and have you given the ship a name?" asks Eric.

"Huh, the name of the ship, it has no name! As hectic as it's been lately, I'm not sure anyone has had time to think about that. However, the other crewmembers include George Lee, you, and that new guy Chuck Johnson."

Very emphatically, Eric shouts, "Who is Chuck Johnson? And when did he join the program?

Professor Mueller pulls into the parking lot where he picked up Eric. "I don't know much about Chuck Johnson. All I know is Raymond Richards introduced him a few months ago as some navigator pilot."

Professor Mueller extends his hand as Eric prepares to exit his vehicle. "Call me tomorrow, my young friend," requests Professor Mueller while he shakes Eric's hand.

Eric starts his car and watches Professor Mueller pull off. He waits a few moments before doing the same. While driving home, the spirit of the Lord keeps echoing in his mind, Psalm 118:23. Eric becomes more obsessed with this scripture as he struggles to remember the words of this text. As he draws closer to his home, another scripture permeates his thoughts. Eric rehearses over and over in his mind; "I the Lord do all these things." However, this verse he knows from Isaiah 45:7. Arriving at home, the first thing Deacon Eric Miller does is head for his study. He has in mind searching for Psalm 118:23, but before doing so, he notices the telephone off the hook and hangs up the receiver. Eric notices the time on the digital display reads 11:45 p.m. Reaching for his Bible, Eric starts silently thanking God. Not realizing it, his thanks turn into praises, and he falls on his knees and begins to pray. The Holy Ghost has him uttering words out loud not in his native vocabulary. As he becomes aware of his actions, he acknowledges his inability to interpret what God has been attempting to teach him since departing from the parking lot. He privately asks God to open his understanding to the scriptures in his mind so that he might do God's will. He quotes Luke 24:45 in a soft and humble tone, "Then opened he their understanding, that they might understand the scriptures." He rises from his knees and sits in his chair. He turns the pages in his Bible, stopping at the book of Psalms.

Before reaching Psalm 118, he recites, "This is the Lord's doing; it is marvelous in our eyes." Deacon Eric Miller recites it several times until he finally reaches the twenty-third verse of Psalm 118. Realizing this was the phrase he was just reciting, Eric rejoices greatly speaking occasionally in an unknown language. Having an unexplainable awareness of what is required of him, he experiences an overwhelming sense of peace and tranquility. He glances at his watch; 11:45 p.m. appears on the display. In disbelief, literally no time has elapsed. He picks up the receiver on his desk phone to illuminate the digital display. The time is indeed 11:45 p.m. Eric Miller is convinced he must journey into space and complete what God has started through him.

Dr. Erica Myers hears the faint sound like an alarm clock and makes an attempt to shut it off, but she quickly realizes that the sound is coming from her watch and not her alarm clock. Erica has spent the night in her big comfortable chair in her living room. The last thing she remembers is finishing a bottle of champagne left by her realtor. She thinks to herself how tired she must have been and wishes she had gone shopping for food. Instead of making a fresh pot of coffee and enjoying some bacon and eggs, she will have to settle for gas station coffee and a bagel. She rises gracefully from the chair and starts toward the bathroom. She suddenly stops, realizing she has not only had a dream but also remembered it for the first time. Turning and walking back to her living room, she retrieves and carries two pieces of luggage to her bedroom, constantly rehearsing the details of her dream as to not forget it. Unzipping the larger of the two, a scent emerges reminding her of her mother and her home. It was her mother's scarf. Closing her eyes and inhaling deeply, she savors its smell and moves it ever so gently across her face. Exhaling, she removes the fabric from her face, down to her neck, and compassionately to her breast. A spine-tingling chill rushes quickly through her body. On the verge of tears, she delicately places the scarf on her unmade bed. Rushing through her luggage searching for cosmetics, Erica murmurs to herself, "I have to unpack my things tonight and get settled in. Oh my God, did they drop off my car?" In a frenzy, Erica rushes through her house out into the garage, her heart pounding, just to spot her car. "Oh thank you, God," she shouts. "Calm down girl and get ready for work." Wide awake now, Erica takes a shower and dresses. Returning to the garage, she starts her car. Reentering the house, she makes out a grocery list but pauses, laughs, and takes note of the fact that she needs just about everything. Using her GPS, Erica enters the address of the Space Agency. Returning to her bedroom, she retrieves her mother's scarf. She wraps it around her neck and returns to the garage. "This is going to be a great day!" she thinks to herself. On the way to work, she is fortunate enough to spot a minimart filling station. She will finally get that long awaited cup of java and a bagel. While just her first day, Dr. Erica Myers gets the warm and secure feeling these journeys to and from work will be pleasant ones. Erica treasures this, her first drive in to her new job. She takes in all the scenery and wonders when the day will arrive that she takes this beauty for granted and traveling to work becomes routine.

Pulling up to the guard shack at the employee entrance gate, a guard stops Erica Myers and checks her credentials.

"Your first day, Dr. Myers?" he asks.

"Yes, sir, it is," she eagerly replies.

Handing her papers back to her he states, "My name is Broderick, Doctor. But people here call me Bo. Put this parking sticker in the lower left-hand side of your windshield and have a nice day."

Smiling, Erica proceeds into the parking lot. Her first thought was to take one of the handicap spots, but she instantly decides against it. When her Minnesota tags expire, she thinks she will just get standard Texas plates. For close to ten years now, she doesn't even carry a cane with her. For all practical purposes, Dr. Erica Myers does not consider herself handicapped. Entering into the building, Erica walks slowly as if taking in the sites, not sure where her office is located. The sometimes shy woman is conscious of other employees watching her, wondering if it's because she walks with a limp, because she is lost, or both. She overhears one young man ask another if she has an injury or if the limp is permanent. The other responds by telling his buddy, she sure is fine. I'll wait before hitting on her in case it's not an injury. Another woman stops to assist her.

"Hi, I'm Betty," pointing to her badge, "Betty Rose. Do you have a badge?

"Oh yes, I do, Betty," retrieving it from her purse and fastening it to her blouse.

"Good morning, Dr. Erica Myers. Let's see, your badge says L215. Take these elevators to the second floor, turn right, and go to the end of the hall. Looks like you're working with the mission director."

"Thank you, Betty. But where are the stairs?"

"Oh, I'm sorry, Dr. Myers. I meant no disrespect," as Betty points toward the stairs.

"Thank you so much, Betty. I hope to see you around."

Making her way to the top of the stairs, Erica can see her office at the end of the hallway. She approaches one of the young men who had previously made a comment about her. As she gets close enough for him to hear her, Erica whispers, "The limp is permanent." A few feet further, Erica enters the doors designated as Office of the Flight Director. Walking in, a middle-aged man standing next to a coffeepot looks up at her.

"Well, good morning. You must be Dr. Myers! Dr. Erica Myers?" The man approaches her and holds out his hand. "I'm David Veil. Welcome to the Space Agency."

Extending her hand to shake his, Erica acknowledges, "Yes, I'm Dr. Myers. Pleased to meet you, Mr. Veil."

"David, just call me David, Dr. Myers. And how would you like for us to address you?" asks David Veil.

"My colleagues call me Erica, but my friends call me Ricky."

"Well, Erica, let's introduce you to the rest of the team," suggests David Veil. Leading the way as Erica follows, Veil continues, "After you meet everyone, I'll show you to your office."

The phone rings in General Westbrook's office. He answers to hear his secretary's voice. "You have a call on line 1, General."

"Thank you, Ms. Hayes," replies General Westbrook.

General Westbrook pushes the lighted button on his phone and lifts the receiver to his ear. "General Westbrook."

"Good morning, General Westbrook, Professor Mueller here. I have that list of crew assignments you requested. Is now a good time for you?"

"Sure thing, Professor. Whatcha got?" asks General Westbrook.

"To make things a little easier for you, I've put together a brief portfolio on each of the three candidates we've chosen. I'd like to fax them over to you if that's okay, General," petitions Professor Mueller.

"That's perfect, Professor. I'll put Ms. Hayes back on the line and she'll give you our fax number. We'll review them and prepare a preliminary report. I'd also like to have them come here so our team doctor can evaluate them. Do you see this as a problem, Professor?"

"Not at all, General Westbrook," answers Professor Mueller. "While I have you in the line, I thought it best that you know one of the crew members by the name of Chuck Johnson has only been with RNR Industries a short time. I do not know much about him personally, but my colleague Raymond Richards says he comes highly recommended. I am currently making arrangements for the trio to be in Houston this Thursday."

General Westbrook asks Professor Mueller to stay on the line so that Helen Hayes can give him instructions as to where to send the documents. He thanks Professor Mueller before putting him on hold. He then asks Helen Hayes to get Walter Kennedy on the line. He further instructs her to hold all his calls as he does not want to be disturbed. Moments later, Helen Hayes informs General Westbrook that Walter Kennedy is on line 1. General

Westbrook informs Walter Kennedy that he will soon have three candidates to investigate. Walter Kennedy in turn informs the general that at this point, both Professor Mueller and Raymond Richards along with their operations appear to be spotless. While on the line with Walter Kennedy, Ms. Hayes quietly tiptoes into General Westbrook's office and softly lays on his desk three folders labeled confidential. She was instructed to also fax these portfolios to Walter Kennedy.

"I've just been handed a set of crew profiles, General Westbrook," states Walter. "I see they have a Chuck Johnson listed."

"Is there a problem, Director Kennedy?" demands General Westbrook as he too opens the folders just handed to him by Ms. Hayes.

"No, sir, General Westbrook. I'll give the results of background checks to you shortly," replies Walter Kennedy before abruptly ending the call.

General Westbrook pulls the phone slowly down from his ear and stares at it a moment before placing the receiver back on the cradle. The haste in which Walter Kennedy ended the call has raised some suspicion. He thinks for a moment about calling Director Walter Kennedy back but thinks to himself it's best to let this thing play itself out. He composes himself and calmly heads out of his office toward the offices of the flight director with the crew portfolios.

With authority, General Westbrook enters the flight director's office. He finds David Veil talking to Dr. Erica Myers outside her new office. Without breaking stride or excusing himself, he demands, "David, I need to see you and Dr. Myers in your office right now." David, looking at Erica, motions for her to follow him to his office. Once the three have gathered into the room, General Westbrook makes another demand, "Please close the door, Doctor, and have a seat." David Veil sits behind his desk, while General Westbrook and Dr. Erica Myers take seats in front of him.

Looking at Dr. Erica Myers, General Westbrook begins, "What do you know about the psychological effects deep space travel could have on astronauts?"

Somewhat taken by surprise, Dr. Myers answers, "There are several factors that come to mind, including the fear of death, being confined in close quarters for long periods, and problems from people with similar backgrounds, General."

"So if you interviewed some candidates, you could determine whether or not they would be compatible with one another and could survive a lengthy journey into deep space?" asks General Westbrook.

"Yes, sir, I would interview them separately, then together. I can group the candidates according to their propensity to coexist with one another."

"Good, Doctor. I will have perspective crew members here for your examination on Thursday."

"General, may I also add that it is my belief that a doctor should also accompany a crew to collect data in real time and to continue to observe the crew's behavior, making sure they maintain their sanity," adds David Veil.

"Understood, David, and I agree. Dr. Myers, make sure you are compatible with these candidates as if you were making the trip as well."

An even more surprised Erica Myers looks at David Veil who is equally shocked by General Westbrook's implication that Dr. Erica Myers could potentially be part of the crew. Standing, General Westbrook lays some folders on the corner of Mr. Veil's desk in front of Dr. Myers. "These folders contain profiles of three men I want you to examine and determine if they are capable of undergoing such a mission together. I know you will want to examine them in person, but I would like a preliminary behavioral assessment by the end of the day Wednesday. Oh yeah, Dr. Myers, welcome to the Space Agency." With this said, General Westbrook leaves the flight director's office.

David Veil looks at Dr. Myers and states, "I think you have your work cut out for you Dr. Myers. Let me know if you need anything."

"I need to know what's happening here, Mr. Veil. I knew my experience as a psychiatrist with interest in deep space flights was important. I was told that my interest in astronomy and deep space navigation was what set me apart for this job. What I wasn't told was that I would possibly be traveling into space."

"Close the door and have a seat, Doctor," instructs Mr. Veil. "This is somewhat news to me as well. In a meeting just yesterday, we found out for certain that a group of scientist and engineers had designed a spaceship capable of traveling at light speeds into outer space. They approached us needing our tracking systems. We were delighted to partner with them, seeing that the Germans and

Soviets might also have a vehicle ready to make that jump. I am aware that General Westbrook wanted someone from our agency to accompany them on the mission. But let's not be hasty. General Westbrook did not say for certain you are going to make the trip."

Erica Myers takes a deep breath and then exhales. She stands and limps slowly toward the door. Then suddenly, she swirls around and heads straight for David Veil as if to hurt him, causing David to push back from his desk. "This is blasted unbelievable!" she shouts with the brightest of smiles on her face while securing the profiles on the corner of David Veils desk. "Wouldn't it be awesome if I had an opportunity to go where no cripple has gone before? I never dreamed this could ever happen to me. If only my dad could see me now. Oh man, pinch me, David. Oh, I mean, Mr. Veil."

"Wow, Doc," says David Veil, as he regains his composure, straightens out his necktie, and positions himself back up under his desk. "You gave me a little scare there, lady. I take it you're up for this?"

"Yes, sir!" blurts out Dr. Myers.

"Then I take it you have some preparation to attend to. I hope you realize this mission is top secret, Dr. Myers. And whatever you do, don't get your hopes up too high as being a member of this crew. Remember, your main objective is to examine the psyche of the RNR Industry crew. And by all means, please just call me David."

Erica Myers rushes out of David Veil's office with all the jubilation and enthusiasm of a teenager about to embark on her first big date. She spends the rest of the day on her laptop entering information about the crewmembers. Her excitement is imputed to the flight director as well, who spends the rest of his day going over the flight plan included in the package Professor Mueller and Raymond Richards left for them.

General Westbrook instructs Helen Hayes to contact Professor Mueller to confirm his crew will be in Houston for an examination on Thursday morning. She needs security clearance and guest badges for them to have upon arrival.

William Kennedy frantically makes attempts to contact Raymond Richards but can only leave voices messages. His messages to Raymond Richards the night before were to confirm the launch was a go, but definitely not to have Chuck Johnson become a member of the crew. Now having seen pictures along with the crew profiles sent from Professor Mueller, he is extremely concerned that any information discovered about Chuck Johnson would definitely expose him as anything but a pilot and navigator. NIA director Walter Kennedy sent him to RNR Industries to gain information and fabricated his credentials as a pilot and navigator in order for him to gain access to the project. He places a call to the Soviet prime minister informing him of this problem. The Soviet prime minister advises Walter Kennedy not to worry and that he will handle the situation.

The telephone rings at Eric Miller's residence, but there is no answer. The caller then calls EM Laboratories. Hearing the phone ring, Eric thinks to himself that on most any other day, he would let the answering machine pick it up. "Eric Miller speaking," he answers.

"Eric Miller, my young friend, this is Professor Mueller. This won't take long. Just wanted to let you know the crew should be in Houston Thursday morning for your preliminary evaluation with the Space Agency's doctor. How long will it take you to load your experiments?"

"Good morning, Professor. The majority of my hardware was installed before I left the hangar months ago. I should have controlware ready by this afternoon and will upload them into the ship's memory core before the day is over. I will call you later tonight at your home. Take care, Professor."

Professor Mueller calls Raymond Richards at his office and informs him that Eric Miller has rejoined the team, that the lists of candidates along with their profiles have been sent to General Westbrook, and that the crew will need to be in Houston Thursday morning. This is great news to Raymond Richards; however, he wants to talk face-to-face with Professor Mueller. Professor Mueller is not quite sure what they are going to discuss, but he does not want to meet at Raymond Richards's RNR Industries office as he suggests. They agree to meet for lunch in a downtown Ann Arbor restaurant at noon.

Eric Miller returns to RNR Industries and stops at the guard gate. He is greeted with a warm welcome and is waved through. He drives straight to the hypership's hangar. Upon entering the hangar, the first person he encounters is George Lee. The two men shake hands and embrace. "I can't tell you how good it is to see you again, Eric Miller," says George.

"The feeling's mutual, George," replies an emotional Eric Miller. Looking at the spacecraft, he continues, "It was not easy walking away from her, George. She is a work of art, G." G was the nickname Eric Miller gave George Lee some time ago. "You had your first cup of coffee yet this morning?"

"Had one on the way in, but I think it's time for another with my friend."

"Let's not finish our brews until we have given this ship a name," suggests Eric.

The two men walk toward the break room in the hangar. The handful of employees who have a security clearance to the hangar greet them warmly as they pass by. A short young black woman leaving the break room as they enter, not paying attention to the pair entering, runs right into Eric.

"Oh, excuse me . . . ," she says. Then noticing it's Eric, she says, "Eric Miller, oh my God, Eric." Very emotional and nearly in tears, she intimately embraces him and holds on to him for nearly a minute.

As she slowly lets him go, Eric responds to her, "It's so good to see you again, Grace. How are you?"

"I am so unbelievably pleased to see you again, Eric. I have missed your godly inspiration and wisdom the past few months. If you had not shown me the truth, I might still be living a lie. Who knows when God would have saved me?" Turning Eric loose, but still holding his hand, Grace directs her attention toward George. "I'm sorry, George, how are you?"

"I'm good, Grace. Thanks for asking," replies George Lee.

"I'll see you later, guys," she says starting to move away but still squeezing Eric Millers hand.

While letting go of her hand, Eric replies, "God bless you, Grace. See ya later."

Grace has just made a fresh pot of coffee. George and Eric pour themselves a cup and take a seat at one of the tables.

"Did you and Grace ever think about, you know, getting together, Eric?" asks George. "It seems as if she really likes you, and you share some of the same religious beliefs."

"I'd be lying to you if I said it never crossed my mind, George. But I was led by the spirit of God to talk to her about the scriptures and not about the two of us. She was troubled about the very subject God gave me to her to speak on. Grace is a gifted engineer and doctor. But enough about Grace, let's talk about our vessel."

"You got it, brother! I take it the name Grace is out," remarks George in a jovial manner.

"Yeah," responds Eric with a smile. "That is a word I associate more with God's unmerited favor. I don't see it as a name for our flying saucer. When I think about our ship, I don't even see a woman's name."

"I think I know what you mean, Eric. I see something cosmic, something mystical, and something relative to the stars."

"Yeah," responds Eric again, "you bring out something that has been in the back of my mind. The heavens have an untold story, and our spacecraft's name could suggest the unveiling of a story. But how do we do that in one word?"

"You say the stars hold untold stories, but is that really true? The Greeks were passionate about creating stories to parallel human emotional realities. Unfortunately, I don't know much about Greek mythology. How about you, Eric?"

"I know a little Greek mythology, George. As they say, I know just enough to be dangerous. I know just enough to believe that your insight has probably given us a name for the ship."

"Then spit it out, man. Don't keep me in suspense," shouts an excited George Lee. "What will be the name of the ship?"

"How about the *Argo Navis*?" whispers Eric before taking a sip of coffee.

"*Argo Navis*, *Argo Navis*, I love it!" shouts George. "Now tell me the story behind this *Argo Navis*. And please, Eric, just the short version."

"Believe me, George, all I can remember from my college study in Greek mythology is short. But simply, the mythical ship Argo carried the Argonauts from Thessaly to Colchis in search of the Golden Fleece."

"Oh man, this is good, Eric. One day you must tell me the whole story." Finishing his coffee and standing, George continues, "Let's go on board. I have some things to show you since you've been away. The technology in the *Argo Navis* is light years ahead of what the boys at the Space Agency could even dream of."

"Who's going to tell Raymond Richards and Professor Mueller the name of the ship?" asks Eric as the men approach the ship.

"You named it, Eric, you tell them," answers George.

George Lee stops at a locker and enters in a code, and the door of the locker opens. He puts on a pair of gloves that Eric has never seen and hands another pair of identical gloves to Eric. Eric puts the gloves on and notices after a few seconds they seem to tighten themselves around his hands like surgical gloves. Seconds later, he hardly knows they are on his hands. He follows George, who is walking up the ramp into the side of the *Argo Navis* toward a closed access hatch. George stretches forth his hand, appears to touch the ship, and walks right through it. Eric is amazed and stands motionless. He suddenly hears George's voice encouraging him to just keep walking through the access hatch even thought is appears to be closed. With his heartbeat racing on the verge of explosion, he likewise enters into the ship. Then he shouts, "Wow!"

It's now 12:30 p.m. Tuesday afternoon, and Professor Mueller has been waiting at the Main Street restaurant for nearly half an hour. Pulling out his cell phone, he dials Raymond Richards's number. Half a second later, he hears the sound of a cell phone ringer. He looks in the direction of the sound just to see Raymond Richards hurrying toward him.

"Sorry I'm late, Professor Mueller. I've been trying to reach Chuck Johnson all morning to inform him of his selection to the crew," explains Raymond Richards as he fumbles with his cell phone. "I also had to take Pat's car to the shop. I noticed she had some front-end damage when she got home from her workout this morning. Someone just tried to call me, but I think I lost them."

"It was probably me, Raymond. Why don't you have a seat and we'll get started. You seem to be a little on edge."

A waitress gives them a menu and asks them if they would like a beverage as they look it over. Both men request hot tea and do not want anything right away. They request that she leave the menus. Moments later, she returns with their beverages and tells them that if they want anything, just let her know.

"Well, Professor, I have been a little on edge since our return from Houston yesterday. In talking with my wife, she thought it best if we just got everything out into the open. You see, Professor, I kept asking you if you had information regarding this mission I was not aware of because I thought you might have discovered a secret I've been holding from you. When General Westbrook agreed so rapidly to accept our proposal, and when you so nonchalantly responded, I felt you knew."

Professor Mueller impatiently asks, "Knew what, Raymond?"

Taking a sip of his tea, Raymond Richards reluctantly continues, "You see, Professor, I was contacted by Director Walter Kennedy in the intelligence agency a few months ago, stating he knew what we were doing and not to tell anyone, even you. He was going to send someone to monitor our operation, and they did. That person is Chuck Johnson."

Without going into any details, Professor Mueller told Raymond Richards he does suspect there are some secrets between them. He also tells Raymond Richards why Eric left the program and that Eric's work while having been compromised was corrected. They are not sure how vast the intrusion spread, and there is strong evidence another ship exists. They are not sure to what extent it was completed. Finally, Professor Mueller insists Raymond Richards to keep him informed on every action from now on, regardless of how insignificant it may seem. Both men along with Eric Miller and George Lee have invested millions of dollars and an infinite amount of time on this project, and a high degree of honesty and respect is demanded. The two men shake hands and decide to question Chuck Johnson. Professor Mueller is going to relay the information about Chuck Johnson to General Westbrook to see what reactions it would produce. Just as Professor Mueller and Mr. Richards decide to order lunch, Professor Mueller's cell phone rings. It is an excited Eric Miller who informs the professor of the ship's name. Professor Mueller smiles and relays the information to Raymond Richards. Neither Professor Mueller nor Raymond Richards can remember the significance of this name, but they know there must be one.

After lunch, Professor Mueller calls General Westbrook from his office and informs him about Chuck Johnson. General Westbrook in turn admits that since talking to Professor Mueller earlier, he knew Director Walter Kennedy was hiding something when he saw the profile of Chuck Johnson. General Westbrook assures Professor Mueller he has no prior knowledge of any indiscretion on the part that Walter Kennedy is solely behind him. General Westbrook hopes Professor Mueller and Raymond Richards made no drastic moves regarding Chuck Johnson until further information about him could be confirmed and at this point realizes he would not be a member of the crew. He also tells them he has considered asking a member of the Space Agency, Dr. Erica Myers, to join the crew.

Professor Mueller contacts Raymond Richards and told him not to disclose any of the information they found on Chuck Johnson to anyone. But thus far, Chuck Johnson's whereabouts remain unknown.

Eric Miller is working in the ship's engineering section when he hears his name called out requesting that he come to the ship's bridge. Not sure how the communication system works, he looks around and replies that he will be there in five minutes. He pauses to marvel at all the technological upgrades George has installed in the ship. George has reengineered all the ship's consoles and panels so that they can be operated using these gloves. All these systems can also be cloaked when not in use. Eric has spent hours reviewing the functionality of these enhancements. He has gotten the hang of using the gloves that operate the systems and can do so from anywhere in the ship. He positions his fingers as if they were touching keys on a standard keyboard, and it makes visible the console entered. The tight fitting membrane gloves are then used to operate that console and seem to have unlimited range. He initiates a lock and cloak command and watches as all the systems on the lower engineering level seem to disappear. He also notices that his watch indicates the time is well past midnight. He walks toward the front center of the ship. Eric pauses at the ladder leading to the upper level. As he touches the ladder, the spirit of the Lord overcomes him, and he drops to his knees. Silently, Eric prays, "Lord God and Father of our Lord and Savior Jesus Christ, I come to you as humbly as I know how. There is no other God but you. You and only you created all things. You are the sovereign God of the universe, and there is none like you. Most importantly, Lord, I thank you for sending your son Jesus Christ and for saving my soul. Oh, God, if it's in your will, bless this mission and its crew, in Jesus's name, amen and amen." Eric proceeds up the ladder to the bridge. The upper level also houses the living quarters, a galley lounge, an infirmary, and a restroom. The ship's entry and exit hatch is also on the upper level. Eric enters the ship's upper level located between the second row of chairs where the engineering and navigation stations are. The pilot and copilot stations are closer together and at the very front of the vessel. George Lee is sitting at the pilot's station, one of four chairs that look more like heavy duty dentist chairs. He has numerous holographic consoles open, running multiple diagnostics. Eric pauses and takes note at the ease and joy George Lee experiences in performing tasks. George then detects Eric's presence.

"Take a seat, Eric," requests George pointing at the copilot's chair to his right. "I need to set you up with voice recognition and engineering level security authentication to all systems. How's everything looking in the basement?"

"The basement huh, I like that," says Eric as he makes himself comfortable in his chair. "The engines seem to be just like I left them, George. But I can't speak for the ship's systems; that's your area." Pausing a second, Eric continues, "George, I had a little chat with Professor Mueller concerning my return to the program. I told him why I left, but I did not tell him of your involvement and that we worked together to rectify these problems."

George stops running his diagnostics and turns toward Eric. "So you think we can trust him? After all, I know you two have history."

"Yes, George, I do trust him. He told me he suspected Raymond Richards of voluntarily working with the National Intelligence Agency. He planned on meeting with him earlier today. I'm hoping he can shed some light on our copilot Chuck Johnson."

"Chuck Johnson!" shouts George. "That clown came along literally the day you left. He reminds me of a washed up drunk who couldn't fly a kite, less known a spaceship. I've never let him on board. Listen, brother. This is a culmination of my life's work. I cannot, I will not, let anything destroy this ship's chance to succeed.

I think it's a bad idea having that dude around. I don't trust him, and I don't want him on my ship." Lowering his head and his voice, George continues, "Man, you are about the only one I trust these days."

"I feel the same way, George. Man, these chairs are really comfortable!"

"They were designed by a friend of mine back on the mainland. They will keep our bodies from shattering under the massive force exerted by your engines. The ship's inertia-dampening systems will also relieve some of these stresses." George turns around in his chair and calls up a console. "Activate voice recognition program, alpha-alpha-one." Then looking at Eric, he continues, "Let's get your voice programmed into the system and assign you security access. Now, Eric, when I give you the signal, state your name, numerical birthday, and city of birth followed by state. Speak slow and clear." George signals Eric to begin.

"Eric Miller, 7-6-55, Detroit, Michigan," recites Eric.

Once finished, George gives Eric his access clearance code. "When you need to access systems with or without the gloves, just speak your system into existence, followed by alpha-alpha-two. Now, what do you say we call it a night? Oh yeah, Grace came by and loaded up the galley for us. She said she'll see you tomorrow."

Erica Myers is so captivated in her work that she does not realize what time it has become. She has been downloading atlas star charts into her computer since noon, having completed the preliminary psychological profiles on the three prospective crewmembers. Shutting down her computer, Erica wonders what kind of navigation systems are on board the ship and dreams of integrating her data into the ship's computer systems. She knows one of the men selected is a navigator and ponders what kind of star charts he will use. Envying the navigator, Dr. Myers prepares to leave for the night, but not before taking another look at the profiles, knowing that General Westbrook will want a thorough evaluation report on Wednesday. One of the candidate's names weighs heavy on her mind, but she is not able to put her finger on it. Packing her briefcase and closing her office door, Dr. Myers heads for the parking garage.

Unlocking her car, entering the vehicle, and starting it up, Erica Myers remembers she still needs to do some grocery shopping but decides it's too late for that now. A hot pizza and a cold pop sound like dinner tonight. Once home, Erica uses the phone book to find a pizza parlor that delivers after midnight and places her order. She takes a quick shower before her meal arrives. Drying her hair, Erica realizes she still has yet to talk to her mother. She starts writing a note to herself to call her mom but is interrupted by the doorbell. Having paid for her pizza, Erica goes into the kitchen to eat, taking the crew's profile folders with her. Eating and thinking, Erica cannot figure out why it is that one of these names seems more familiar to her than the others, and for what reason. She knocks herself for not taking the complete folder General Westbrook gave her as there were pictures of each subject. That might have jogged her memory some but figures she will meet the trio soon, and maybe then what's in her subconscious mind will surface. Getting a good night rest in her own bed sounds like the best therapy she can prescribe.

Wednesdays are normally fasting days for Eric Miller, and he cannot think of a better reason than a maiden voyage into the heavens to spend this day in prayer and supplication. But first, he must attend a 9:00 a.m. meeting at RNR Industries. Professor Mueller and Raymond Richards plan to make a formal announcement concerning the upcoming events surrounding the soon-to-be-not-so-secret project and the Space Agency's involvement.

Employees from Eric Miller's EM Laboratories, Professor Mueller's Mueller Engineering, and RNR Industries owned and operated by Raymond Richards have gathered in the main auditorium at RNR Industries. Raymond Richards begins with a speech thanking everyone for their amazing contributions and accomplishments. He emphatically insists that their achievements will infuse new life into their combined disciplines. He challenges them to come up with a name for a new company born of this venture. The new company will produce spacecrafts for both governmental and commercial uses. The audience responds favorably to these statements with cheers and applause. Raymond Richards then announces the names of the three crew members who will make this historic journey. He asks that they stand and be recognized for their efforts. Eric Miller and George Lee stand, but there is no indication that Chuck Johnson is present. This does not discourage anyone present. George makes a remark to Eric that Johnson must have gotten drunk yesterday and needed to sleep it off. Raymond Richards then introduces Professor Mueller. Professor Mueller reveals the name of the ship, the *Argo Navis*. He also tells the audience that a preliminary launch date for the *Argo Navis* will be Friday night under the cover of darkness. The Space Agency will be tracking the flight and have one of their doctors on board to monitor the crew's performance. Professor Mueller insists that this mission will be a phenomenal success and will have an impact on our society like no other technological advancement in the planet's history. He concludes by asking everyone to pray for the crew and this venture.

Raymond Richards and Professor Mueller invite everyone to the ship's hangar where they have provided coffee, juice, and other beverages, as well as donuts, cookies, bagels, and fruit. It is the first time all employees from each of the companies involved in the manufacturing of the saucer come together. It is also the first time most have seen the finished ship. Everyone is enjoying themselves tremendously and has taken time to wish Eric and George a safe trip. Raymond Richards's secretary likewise congratulates Eric Miller and George Lee before handing each of them packages including reservations for a one night stay at the Hilton Clear Lake Hotel, about seven miles from Ellington Airport, and their itineraries and contacts at the Space Agency. Then directing her attention to George Lee, she informs them the hangar crew will have RNR Industries' private jet ready by five o'clock, as he will pilot them to Houston. Everything else they would need is in their packages. She gives both George and Eric hugs and tearfully wishes them well.

"I wonder why Raymond Richards and Professor Mueller are taking a commercial flight to Houston on Monday?" asks George Lee.

"Professor Mueller hates small aircraft," says Eric. He then excuses himself so that he may go home and spend the remainder of the day in prayer. He calls Pastor Walls, leaving a message on his answering machine informing him that he will not be attending Bible class tonight and probably won't be home Saturday for their weekly basketball game. He humbly requests Pastor Walls and his wife, Sandy, to pray for him this week but does not divulge any details as to why. When Pastor Walls arrived home, he retrieved Eric's message. Together with his wife, they pray a general prayer for Deacon Eric Miller, realizing Eric did not mention exactly what he wanted them to pray for. Sandy expresses concern for their good friend, but Pastor Walls insists he is only concerned about their ball game. Deep down inside, Sandy knows her husband is really just as concerned as she is. After their dinner, Sandy asks her husband if he knows anything she does not. All he tells her is that Eric and his fate are on a parallel course.

Dr. Myers has spent all day in the office reviewing information she received relative to RNR Industries and their proposal. It has been a challenge for her throughout the day to think of interviewing a crew for a confined and extended journey in deep space. Suddenly and unexpectedly, Dr. Myers's thoughts shift to her mother. While there is still daylight and it is fresh on her mind, Dr. Erica Myers picks up the phone on her desk and dials her mother's number. Between the second and third ring, Mrs. Myers answers the phone, "Hello, Myers residence."

To Erica's delight, she answers, "Hello, Mother. It's your daughter, Erica. How are you doing?"

A very surprised Mrs. Myers responds, "Ricky, oh how I've been expecting to hear from you, my dear. Have you gotten all settled in? How's the new job? Do you like what you're doing? What's the weather like down there . . . ?"

"Hold on now, Mother, slow down. One question at a time," begs Erica. "I've been literally living out of my suitcases, the weather is very warm, and as you might imagine, working for the Space Agency is a dream come true. I've got my first assignment, but it is classified."

"Oh, dear, I'm so glad to hear your voice."

"Same here, Mother. You know, I've been thinking about you so much the last . . ."

Before Erica can finish, there is an interruption as someone else has called her mother. "Erica, dear, let me put you on hold a moment."

Before Erica can respond, her mother has taken the other call. Erica waits for a good three to four minutes before the line gets disconnected. She tries to redial several times, only to get her mother's recorded message. Finally, she decides to leave her mother a voice message, including her new work phone number and home number. Erica knows she must leave work on time to get some much needed groceries, make a nice dinner, and get a good night's sleep.

Eric arrives back at RNR Industries with a small travel bag and proceeds straight to hangar 13. The hangar bay doors are open, and the RNR Industries main executive jet sits just outside. The flight operations office is located inside the hangar. Eric opens the door and finds George there filing a flight plan. He greets Eric with a handshake and hug before asking, "How you doing, my man? We're all fueled up and just about ready to go. I just want to double check weather conditions. Oh yeah, I got a note from Raymond Richards informing us to go ahead without Chuck Johnson. No tears here!"

"Is there anything I can do to help?" asks Eric.

"Nah, brother, if you have prayed for us, that's all I could ask," replies George. Pointing to his bag on the floor, George continues, "Why don't you put our bags on board. I'll be there in two minutes.

"You got it, G," replies Eric with a big grin on his face. Eric leaves the operations office with both their bags, boards the plane, and stores their belongings. He takes a seat and puts his hands to his face in a prayerful fashion. "Oh bless us, Lord, bless us."

Two minutes later, George enters the plane and secures the hatch. He turns to enter the cockpit and demands that Eric takes second chair. "Buckle up for safety, brother, buckle up." The ground crew pulls the jet out onto the runway apron and disconnects their gear. Seconds later, they signal they are ready to go. George fires up the jet's twin engines and radios the control room to transfer him to the tower. An air traffic controller gives George clearance to depart. Without any further discussion, George whips the craft onto the main runway and speeds away. George puts the plane into a rapid climb and within seconds rises above the clouds. "Better get used to this. Just think, in the time it took us to liftoff until now, we could be halfway to the moon in the *Argo Navis*. I can't wait. We'll travel here and there and somewhere."

"Somewhere?" asks Eric.

"Yeah, man. I can't navigate outer space, can you?"

"You got a point, G. I hope whoever is going to be joining us from the Space Agency is also a navigator, or it could be one quick trip."

The flight to Houston seems to be rather short. The aircraft and its occupants land at Ellington Airport. They lock down the jet and take a taxi to Hilton Clear Lake Hotel. They check into their rooms and put their bags away. Eric calls George on the room phone, and they decide to meet in fifteen minutes at the hotel's restaurant. The two travelers relax, discuss the events that will take place tomorrow, and take their time enjoying a good meal.

"I was reading in our packages that we are to meet a Dr. Myers," explains Eric. "I wonder what would happen if one of us should fail our physicals, or even worse, if Dr. Myers is not a medical doctor but a shrink?"

"You know it's funny you should say that," adds George. Ever since I found out Ray Richards and Professor Mueller were seeking assistance from the Space Agency, I wondered when someone would say what we were attempting was crazy!"

After finishing their meals, Eric pays for the bill, and the two head back to their respective rooms. "Tell me once again why we are here, Eric. Wouldn't it have been easier for them to come to Michigan?" asks George.

"It's God's will we are here. It's our fate, George," explains Eric.

"That's not helping me much!" replies George.

"That's all I got, George," says Eric with a smile as he swipes the entry card to his room. "Good night, G." Eric showers, and as in most nights before retiring, he takes time to read some scriptures from his Bible and pray. As Eric starts his prayer, he acknowledges God for who he is then thanks God for protecting him throughout the day. He asks God to lead him and to guide him through this mission if it's within his divine will and purpose. He believes that if God does not bless him and his crew, they will not survive. For the next few minutes, he meditates, attempting to absorb whatever the spirit of the Lord gives him. Upon rising off his knees, he climbs into bed and returns to his Bible. He is confident that God will direct him to a verse. He finds himself in the book of St. John. Ten and twenty-six comes to his mind, so he turns to chapter 10 and reads verse 26. "But ye believe not, because ye are not of my sheep, as I said unto you." It comes to Eric's mind that this was one of the scriptures God gave him as he first ministered to Grace. The words "Ye believe not, because ye are not of my sheep" keep running through Eric's mind. Unable to grasp what God is trying to show him, he closes up his Bible, turns out the lights, and goes to sleep.

George Lee, Eric Miller, and Erica Myers all wake up before dawn. George makes a pot of coffee and then showers. He gets dressed and then verifies he has every schematic and blue print they have on the saucer's design. George then asks himself a series of both technical and nontechnical questions his audience could pose to him and then answers them. Suddenly, George considers the possibility that his interrogators might want information of a more personal nature. Musing over this causes George to become anxious and uneasy. He decides to take an early morning walk. Eric Miller, waking up from his sleep, knows this mission will define his career. He mysteriously believes this mission is critical to mankind. Eric spiritually believes God will somehow use him to minister to others. Eric is completely confident that God will give him the strength, knowledge, and courage to perform what is set before him. He thanks and praises God for allowing him to be used, as he prepares to take a shower. Eric remembers how Christ prayed three times to God before going to the cross. Stepping into the shower, he prays to God that if he must die on this mission, may his crewmates be spared. The water from the shower blends with his tears. Eric spends more time showering and getting dressed than usual. Still early, he decides to leave his room and take a walk. The sun has not yet risen. He has always found peace in meditating and watching the stars. Erica Myers, so full of anxiety over the interviews she must conduct, is unable to concentrate on anything else. Staring out of her bedroom window into the early morning sky, a chill comes over her realizing that in her lifetime, she could see these same stars from a totally different perspective. Dr. Myers wants to get into the office with plenty of time to prepare for her interviews. Erica feels like she is preparing for a blind date. Her mind goes back to a show she once watched as a kid called *The Dating Game*. One girl asking three men questions without the luxury of seeing them. Erica showers and gets dressed. She gets into her car and begins her commute to work. Driving along, Erica laughs reflecting how her intentions were to make breakfast, but her focus on her job overrides her intentions. Thank God, she thinks to herself, for that convenience store.

Sitting on a bench outside the hotel, Eric Miller hears a familiar voice speak to him, "Rough night, Eric?" He looks around to see

George Lee approaching. "Have I asked you why we had to come to Houston?" asks George.

"Indeed you have, my friend," replies Eric.

"And what was your answer?" asks George.

"I believe I told you that it's God's will we are here," says Eric as he put his arm around the shorter George Lee. "If it's any consolation, I'm very nervous too. I noticed a convenience store a few blocks away last night as we approached the hotel. What do you say we walk there and grab some coffee and bagels?"

"Sounds good, my man."

The duo walks to the gas station and talks about their mission. They are concerned that Chuck Johnson is not with them and that neither Professor Mueller nor Raymond Richards has given them an explanation. They hope that what seems to be a conspiracy against the successful completion of their journey is nothing at all. As they arrive at the gas station, Eric notices a woman drive up with no intention of purchasing gasoline. The woman parks her car on the side of the convenience store just ahead of them. He and George get to the entrance of the building just steps ahead of the woman. While George seems impervious to her presence, Eric takes note to her having a slight but noticeable limp. It's not until Eric steps in front of George to open the door for her that George takes notices. They say good morning to her, and she acknowledges.

George and Eric select bagels and watch the woman attend to her caffeine. "You always spot the ladies, man," remarks George. "I want to grow up to be just like you."

Winking at George, Eric replies, "Keep practicing, G. You'll get there one day."

George and Eric patiently wait their turn and get coffee, just behind the woman with the limp. She smiles and whispers a thank you to them, looking in Eric's direction. After paying for their breakfast, they leave the store and say nothing for a few minutes. Then George breaks the silence.

"It's really a shame that someone so attractive could have such a handicap. I wonder how many dates she's lost."

"I was thinking kind of the opposite," reflects Eric. "How many guys lost an opportunity to be with a great woman? Just makes you count your blessings, you know?"

"I know that's right," agrees George as they enter into the lobby of the hotel. They find the continental breakfast stand is now open. They sit and quietly enjoy their food. "I'm going to grab my briefcase and notebook. Meet you back here in thirty minutes?"

"That's fine," replies Eric. "I think I'll try calling Professor Mueller again. He should be up now. I want to find out if there is any word concerning Chuck Johnson. I can't imagine what might be going on."

Thirty-five minutes later, Eric arrives back in the lobby where George has called for transportation to the Space Agency. He tells George as they leave the lobby that he could not reach Professor Mueller.

Dr. Myers arrives at the agency and like the day before is the first in the office. She sets out a series of papers she will use to perform a psychiatric evaluation on the mission's crew. She giggles and speaks out loud wondering if she should first conduct the survey on herself. Dr. Erica Myers's phone rings, startling her. Who could this be, she thinks to herself as she answers the phone. "Good morning, Dr. Erica Myers speaking. May I help you?"

"Good Morning, Dr. Myers, General Westbrook here. Please come to my office."

General Westbrook hangs up the phone before Dr. Myers can respond. Her heartbeat races at the apparent sense of urgency General Westbrook's summons produced. The only thing Erica can think of as she hurries to General Westbrook's office is that she is being pulled from conducting the interviews. How quickly the thrill of victory has turned into the agony of defeat. Ms. Helen Hayes, General Westbrook's secretary, is not in yet, so Dr. Myers proceeds to the general's door which is open. She knocks, "Excuse me, General, you wanted to see me?"

"Yes, Dr. Myers, I do. Come in and have a seat," says General Westbrook. "I know you have been here just a few days, and we have a tough assignment."

"I realize that, sir, and I'm grateful for the opportunity. I'm honored you have selected me, and I will do whatever is asked of me," replies Dr. Myers. Erica is careful not to mention being taken off this assignment.

"I'm glad you feel that way, Dr. Myers . . . ," continues General Westbrook.

Erica closes her eyes bracing herself for what General Westbrook will say next.

". . . Because I'm also appointing you to the role of navigator on this mission. I know you have worked on deep space navigation as part of your postgraduate studies. How long will it take you to prepare?"

Knowing this validates her joining the crew, Dr. Myers reiterates, "You want me to be the navigator on this mission, sir?"

"Yes, Dr. Myers. Is that a problem?" asks General Westbrook.

"No, sir, not at all," responds an elated Dr. Myers.

"Very good, Doctor. I look forward to reviewing your psychiatric evaluations later. That's all," says General Westbrook. "You're dismissed."

Erica Myers quickly leaves General Westbrook's office, waving her arms and smiling from ear to ear. She stops in the hallway, closes her eyes, and pinches herself just to make sure she is not dreaming. She suddenly wonders what happened to the third crew member who was supposed to navigate the ship but thinks it's best not to question. He would have told me if he wanted me to know, she thinks. Erica reflects how ironic it is she was modifying her navigation program and space charts.

Eric Miller and George Lee arrive at the Space Agency an hour before their scheduled appointment. The men exit their taxi and stand in front of the building.

Exhaling, George Lee looks at Eric Miller and considers, "This time next week, it will all be over."

Stretching forth his arm in the direction of the building, motioning for George Lee to lead the way, Eric acknowledges, "Yeah, G. One way or another, that's true."

Walking slowly toward the building's visitor entrance, George continues, "Are you implying this time next week we could be dead?"

Looking back at George, Eric answers, "In that case, it will be all over for you."

"Hey, man, what you trying to say?"

Opening the door for George, Eric recants, "Forget it man, what do I know?"

The duo approaches the receptionist's desk, and Eric noticing her nameplate politely states, "Good morning, Ms. Devereaux. I am Eric Miller and this is George Lee. We have a nine o'clock appointment with Dr. Myers. Should we sign in and wait somewhere?"

"Sure," replies Ms. Devereaux, handing them their visitor passes. "Just sign the register and have a seat in the waiting area. I'll ring Dr. Myers's office. I'm sure she in her office already."

As Eric and George walk to the waiting area to have a seat, George whispers to Eric, "Did the receptionist say Dr. *Erica* Myers?"

"I caught that too, George!"

"For you that's probably a good thing, but for me that could be disastrous."

"Don't forget, I'm nervous too, George."

"Yeah, but at least you know how to handle women."

"You got a point there, G."

Elizabeth Devereaux dials Dr. Myers's extension. There is no answer so Ms. Devereaux leaves a short message stating her nine o'clock appointments have arrived early. Ms. Devereaux reflects back on how earlier this week two other men from Michigan were here, and they too were early. The first pair was older than these two guys. Her curiosity leads her to call her partner in crime, Helen Hayes. "Helen, this is Liz in the lobby. What do you know about two guys here to see Dr. Myers? Are they related to the same guys who were here on Monday?"

Having just arrived and rushed to get the phone, Helen answers nearly out of breath, "They're not relatives, but they're from the same organization."

"I can see they're not blood relatives, girlfriend. What's the word up there?"

Whispering ever so softly, Helen Hayes expounds, "To make a long story short, the older guys owned factories in Michigan and have made some kind of spaceship. I believe the two down there now are the ones who will pilot it into deep space. I got to go right now. Call me when you're ready for a break. And oh yeah, you can't even whisper this to anyone girl. The general will eat me alive."

"Okay, Helen. I got to go too. I have Dr. Myers on the line."

"Lobby, Ms. Devereaux."

"Ms. Devereaux, this is Dr. Myers."

"Yes, Dr. Myers, how are you?"

"Fine, Ms. Devereaux, thanks for asking."

"I take it you received my message concerning your guest?" asks Ms. Devereaux.

"Yes, I did thanks. I will be down to get them in fifteen minutes. I was not expecting them so soon. Will you relay the message?" instructs Dr. Myers.

"Not a problem, Doctor," says Ms. Devereaux. The two women hang up the phone. Ms. Devereaux calmly walks over to the lounge where Eric Miller and George Lee are sitting, informing them that Dr. Myers will be down in roughly fifteen minutes. They feel fortunate to have a few extra moments to collect themselves.

Meanwhile, Dr. Myers sits nervously at her desk. The fifteen minutes is really meant to give her enough time to compose herself. She wonders what message she will send to her guest should she go down early, late, or right on time. Impulsively, she rises up and walks toward the elevator. "Oh my God, what am I doing?" she thinks after pushing the elevator down button. Will they think I can't walk up or down the stairs? She then turns and walks toward the stairs. Before taking the first step, Dr. Myers envisions falling down the stairs. She holds on to the handrails as if her life depended on it. In the background, she hears the bell signaling the arrival of the elevator on the second floor and nearly falls. Erica stops and looks around to see if anyone is watching her. "Come on girl, get it together," she tells herself. As she approaches the receptionist's desk, Ms. Devereaux points toward the lounge. Both men having their backs to the desk do not sense her approaching. When Dr. Myers gets to within vocal range, she politely introduces herself. "Good Morning, I'm Dr. Myers."

Hearing a woman's voice speak to them, Eric Miller and George Lee turn around and stand. When the three see one another's faces, they immediately reflect back to their encounter at the convenience store earlier that morning. Mounting anxiety causes Dr. Myers to rapidly sit down next to where Eric Miller is standing. The stunned scientists are speechless. Eric and George look at each other as if to say "what next." Eric then breaks the silence by introducing himself.

"I'm Eric Miller," he proclaims. Then pointing to George, "And this is my partner George Lee. Please forgive our astonishment, Dr. Myers, but we had no idea who you were when we saw you this morning." And in a more relaxed tone, Eric admits, "There was going to be a third member of our crew, but as of this morning, it is just the two of us."

Having steadied herself somewhat, Dr. Myers declares, "I likewise gave it no thought that the courteous gentlemen I engaged this morning were my crewmates."

Eric Miller and George Lee look at each other, surprised by Dr. Myers's statement. "Did we hear you correctly refer to yourself as our crewmate, Dr. Myers?" asks George. "We figured someone from the Space Agency would be joining us but . . ."

"But a crippled woman," insinuates Dr. Myers.

George apologetically injects, "That's not at all what I meant, Doctor." Quickly turning to Eric, he gestures with his face and hands for assistance.

"I'm not sure who we expected would be joining us, Dr. Myers, but it is our understanding that you are a psychologist. We were hoping someone from the Space Agency would join us that had knowledge in space navigation, especially in light of the absence of our colleague who was to be our navigator." Then changing the subject, Eric reaches down to assist Dr. Myers from her chair and adds, "This morning, George thought your limp was from a recent slide into second base!"

Standing, Dr. Myers confesses, "I'm sorry, guys. I seem to get defensive when someone says they are surprised about me." Directing her attention to George, she pleads, "So please pardon my behavior, Mr. Lee. I am intrigued by all that is transpiring, and I am still very nervous."

"Please call me George, Dr. Myers. And may I ask what your first name is?"

"Let me start over," says a blushing Dr. Myers. Extending her hand to George, she says, "My name is Erica, Dr. Erica Myers. My friends call me Ricky, and I hope you will too." She turns to Eric and likewise shakes his hand. "Let's go up to my office, shall we?" On the way to the stairs, she reveals that she has also studied interstellar navigation and just today was informed she would be part of the crew.

Feeling more confident, Dr. Erica Myers escorts her guest and crewmates up the stairs and to her office. On the way, she informs them that she is not an astronaut and has not yet completed her first week with the agency. She believes General Westbrook selected her for this mission because of her knowledge in deep space astronomy and high velocity navigation. George and Eric try to remain calm in spite of the unsettling information Dr. Myers is nonchalantly supplying them. Eric and George are also concerned that Dr. Myers is somehow confidently aware that Chuck Johnson has been scrubbed from this mission. They arrive in her office and have a seat. She gives them a document to read and asks that they reply to the questions at the end. She tells them that it is the written part of their psychological evaluation. She will return to give them each an oral evaluation and then chat as a group. Eric and George quickly finish their assignment and quietly wait for Dr. Myers's return. Thirty minutes later, she returns, looks over their work, and asks George if he wouldn't mind being the first one to take the oral evaluation. A very excited George accepts and gestures to Eric as if to say the woman selected me first! Dr. Myers asks Eric if he didn't mind waiting outside her office and directs him to a coffee pot in the break room at the end of the hall. Eric politely excuses himself.

Dr. Myers closes her door and gracefully takes her seat behind her desk. "You don't mind if I call you George, do you, Mr. Lee?"

"Not at all, Dr. Myers," answers George Lee with a big smile.

"Now then, George, tell me a little about yourself, where you were born and raised, your educational background, and any religious or spiritual preferences or persuasions. And please call me Erica."

"Well, Erica, I was born in China but raised in San Francisco. For some reason, my parents wanted my birthplace to reflect our homeland. I went from grade school through college in California. I earned my doctor's degree in Aerospace Engineering from the University of California nearly twenty years ago. I've done research work in China and here in the United States before getting this gig with RNR Industries designing a spaceship, which I might add has been my life's ambition. I am also a test pilot at RNR. As far as religion goes, most people don't believe that Chinese folks can be Christians, but that's how I was raised. I myself have not been to church in some time, but I do believe in God and Jesus Christ. How am I doing, Doc?" asks George with a smile.

Returning the smile, Erica replies, "Just fine, George, you're doing just fine. Tell me a little about your personal life, if you don't mind."

Readjusting himself in his chair, George slowly continues, "Well, this is where the story gets sad, Doc. I have dated numerous girls from Asians to Caucasians but just never seem to meet anyone interested enough in me, or vise versa, to settle down with. Dating seems to be as far as I can get. What about you, Doc, have you ever been married?"

"So I assume you believe I'm not married now, is that correct?" asks Dr. Myers.

In a defensive tone, George quickly replies, "I just didn't see a ring on your finger, so I assumed you were single, Dr. Myers. That's all."

"That's very observant of you, George. No, I have never been married. What about friends, George?" asks Dr. Myers, as she continues to take notes as George talks.

"Mostly all my friends are my colleagues. One of my good friends lives on the mainland and assisted in the design of the ship. Since working on this project, however, Eric and I have become good friends. Other than that, I really don't have a social life."

"Do you and Eric agree on everything?" asks Dr. Myers.

"No one agrees on everything, Doc, but we respect each other's opinion."

"I have one final question, George. As a test pilot, how often do you think about death?"

"About as often as I think about getting into a car accident every time I get into my car," replies George. "It's there, but I don't think about it. If I did, that might take away my edge. I don't have a death wish either, if you were wondering."

"Thank you, George. I think that will be all for now," concludes Dr. Myers. "Please have a seat outside and send in Eric Miller for me."

While waiting for Eric Miller to come into her office, Dr. Myers switches folders and prepares to take notes on Eric. "Come on in Eric. Close the door and have a seat. You don't mind if I call you Eric, do you?"

Eric Miller politely answers, "not at all, Dr. Myers, if I may call you Erica?"

"Fair enough, Eric. Now then," continues Dr. Myers, "tell me a little about yourself, where you were born and raised, your educational background, and any religious or spiritual preferences or persuasions."

"Well, Erica, I thank God for allowing me to be in the position I am today. Without him, I would be nothing. I attend the Grace of God Church in Ypsilanti, Michigan, where I also live. I was born into this physical world in Detroit, Michigan. I was raised and went to school in one of the suburbs of Detroit called Inkster. I attended undergraduate school at the University of Michigan majoring in Nuclear Engineering with a minor in Nuclear Physics. I eventually earned a doctorate in High-Energy Physics from the same institution, writing my thesis on antimatter energy. I owe a lot of my education to Professor Hans Mueller, whom you might have already met. I was born again into the body of Christ in Ypsilanti, Michigan, over twenty years ago. I desire to learn everything there is to know about God and his purpose for saving me."

"So you spent your entire life in Michigan?" asks Dr. Myers.

"No, not exactly," replies Eric. "For about eighteen months when I was in grade school, my family lived in a little town in Iowa. My father's job transferred us there, but it was difficult for us, so we moved back to Michigan."

Dr. Myers starts to nervously shuffle around the profile papers, dropping a few pages on the floor and appearing disoriented.

"Are you all right, Erica?" asks Eric.

Not looking directly at Eric, a visibly shaken Erica states, "Yes, I'm fine. Just give me a few seconds here to get these papers back in order. Please continue."

"Well, I do believe that's about it, Erica. Have you lived in Texas all your life?" inquires Eric.

"No, Eric. I actually just moved here from Minnesota. Believe it or not, this is my first week at the Space Agency." Regaining her composure, Erica pushes her chair back from her desk and stands. Smiling and finally looking at Eric, she remarks, "I think I have enough for right now, Mr. Miller. Will you excuse me a moment?"

Dr. Myers rushes out of the office and tells a waiting George Lee she is going to the ladies room and that he can have a seat in her office with Eric. Not knowing what has just transpired, George reenters the room.

"Well, that's over," cites George Lee as he pulls out a chair and sits next to Eric. "What do you think will happen next?"

"I'm not really sure, George. I believe I might have said something to upset Dr. Myers, but I'm not sure what it was!" says Eric.

"What was the last thing you were talking about?" asks George.

A puzzled Eric, looking down, recalls, "We were talking about where we were raised, and that's when she seemed to get upset."

"Well, if that's all that was said, it might not have nothing to do with you, my man," comforts George. "On her way out, she said she was headed for the ladies room. Maybe she just had to go!"

"Yeah, and maybe I said something that triggered some bad memory and she is crying or something, yah know. Plus, she called me Mr. Miller before she left. What suddenly happened to Eric?"

"Look, my man, I wouldn't worry about it. Let's hit that coffee pot before it's all gone," suggests George.

George and Eric walk outside Dr. Myers's office toward the break room for a fresh cup of coffee. They stand around the coffee station a few minutes as people walk by, everyone smiling and speaking. George and Eric casually return to Dr. Myers's office. George closes the door behind them looking to see if Erica Myers is nearby. He moves close to Eric and whispers, "Eric, when we were down in the lobby, Erica did not seem to be expecting a third person. When she returns, I plan to ask her about it. What do you think, brother?"

"I'm not sure, G. Something's not right. Dr. Myers definitely seems to know more that we do." Taking a seat and pausing for a moment, Eric continues, "She might know Johnson won't be joining us, but she might not know why. I would like to know both, but I don't want to put Dr. Myers on the spot. Let's wait until we can talk to either Professor Mueller or Raymond Richards." Rising and opening the door, Eric concludes, "You good with that?"

"I'm good with that, brother," replies George.

Meanwhile, Dr. Myers exits the ladies room, calmer than when she entered. Erica's suspicion concerning one of the profiles has all but been confirmed, and it involves Eric Miller. She is embarrassed by her reactions and not certain how to proceed. She has concluded, however, that her actions were not professional and must apologize to both Eric and George, but especially Eric. Just outside the ladies room, she bumps into General Westbrook about to enter the men's room.

"How are the crew interviews going, Dr. Myers?" asks General Westbrook.

"I've done both the written and the oral exams but have not had time to put anything in writing yet sir. One seems to be a type A personality, while the other . . . ,"

"Just tell me this, Doctor," interrupts General Westbrook, "do you foresee there being a problem with either of these men and yourself coexisting in confined quarters in deep space? Do you think your combined personalities would affect the success of this mission?"

"No, sir, General."

General Westbrook pressing his hand on the men's room door turns to Dr. Myers and affirms, "Carry on, Doctor."

Erica Myers takes her time returning to her office, contemplating how she will approach Eric and George. She stops at the coffee station, aware that her shipmates are waiting for her. Erica debates whether she should apologize to Eric or watch how things develop and take it from there. This is the second time today she has lost her composure and desperately needs to make sure it does not happen again. Dr. Myers's professional training leads her to believe she should not make any excuses and reenters her office as if nothing has happened. "Sorry to keep you guys waiting, now, where were we?"

Neither George nor Eric answers, both believing Dr. Myers was making a statement as opposed to asking a question. Erica positions herself behind her desk, pulls her chair up, and realizes neither man has responded to her. She shuffles some papers around buying some time to determine how to resume her interviews. Dr. Myers is taken by surprise by a knock on her door. She looks up as George and Eric also position themselves to view Dr. Myers's visitor. Her boss, David Veil, enters the room with another man.

"Excuse me, Dr. Myers, but I wanted you to meet one of our colleagues, William Rodgers," interrupts David Veil while pretending he doesn't notice she has guests. "Bill, I want you to meet the newest member of our staff, Dr. Erica Myers. Dr. Myers has been chosen to join the crew from Michigan testing their hyperspeed spacecraft. Mr. Rodgers is the chief scientist at the Marshall Space Flight Center. He has been assisting me over the last few days setting up the former Apollo mission control room to track your mission."

"Pleased to meet you, Mr. Rodgers," declares Dr. Myers extending her hand.

With an outstretched hand, shaking Dr. Myers's hand, Mr. Rodgers persists, "Just call me Bill, Dr. Myers."

Turning her head in the direction of her guests, Dr. Erica Myers continues; "Mr. Rodgers and Mr. Veil, I would like to introduce you to my crewmates George Lee and Eric Miller. George and Eric, this is my boss David Veil and of course William Rodgers." George and Eric stand and exchange greetings and handshakes.

Without delay, Bill Rodgers suggests, "So I understand that you two gentlemen not only are making the trek into outer space but are the two main architects of this vessel. When you get a moment, I would love to show you how we plan on tracking you and pick your brains a little at the same time."

George Lee anxiously interrupts, "Dr. Myers, do you mind if I went with Mr. Rodgers to see the old Apollo Mission control room? I have always wanted to see that."

"Not at all, George," replies Dr. Myers with a smile. "Just have him back by lunch time, Bill."

George grabs his briefcase, and he along with Bill Rodgers and David Veil rushes out of Erica's office like a kid heading for the candy store. Little do Rodgers and Veil know that George loves to talk about his spaceship.

"I get the impression your boss and Mr. Rodgers actually had meeting George and I in mind when they entered your office, Erica," states Eric breaking the silence.

"I'm sure that's what they wanted, Eric," declares Erica with a smile. The two look at each other for a few seconds, not saying a word. Both stare deeply at each other. Then Erica closes her office door and sits in the chair previously occupied George and asks Eric to sit also. Pulling her dress down around her knees, Erica comments in a more serious tone, "I must confess, Eric, that I feel a strange closeness to you and George, and more so toward you."

Looking directly at Erica and sitting on the edge of his chair, Eric proclaims, "I can't explain it either, Erica. When you left the office during our interview, I thought I had said something to upset you. When you did not call me by my first name, I felt really bad and could not explain it. Then you reentered the room, I said to myself she really did have to go to the little girl's room. And from that moment until now, I can't stop looking at you and wonder what it is about you that is so familiar."

"Eric, would you please continue to tell me about yourself? I promise this is off the record. This is not part of my psychiatric profile on you. I'm just curious. We are going to be confined together for some time, and I'd like to know a little more about the men I could be spending my last days with," expresses Erica.

Eric Miller lives for the moment to talk about his life and how God changed it. He prays for and believes the Lord will provide him with an opportunity to witness to people destined to be saved. Now that he and Dr. Myers are alone, he believes this is the chance to plant a seed in her and prays it takes root. For the next hour, Eric explains how his undergraduate college days were filled with more fun and partying than books. By his junior year, he had taken an interest in high-energy physics taught by Professor Mueller. Professor Mueller convinced him to develop his interest in this discipline and to exploit it. His doctoral thesis was in matter-antimatter energy and containment. Ironically enough, his father's death left him enough money, along with the assistance of a federal grant, to build a laboratory and fully develop his theories. During his father's funeral, however, he became very interested in the eulogy and message preached by his father's pastor. He remembers the minister telling his congregation that his father was saved from God's wrath and judgment, and we should not mourn for him as others mourn, who do not have this same assurance. Eric says the minister then tells them that God had predestinated his father, called him into God's program, justified him, and glorified him according to Romans 8:30. Eric continues by saying this was a type of seed that had been planted in him. He had been impregnated and didn't even know it. He explains that the words were very difficult for him to comprehend and nearly impossible to believe, yet there was this driving force that caused him to start studying the Bible and verify if there was any validity and truth to what he had heard. He regularly attended Bible classes and services where he met another young minister by the name of Elder Michael Walls. The then Elder Walls was different from some of the other ministers there because he related to him. He liked jazz music and sports. They hit it off almost instantly. Elder Walls would laugh at him and tell him that if he was predestined to be in God's plan, there was nothing he could do to get out of it. And if he was not predestined from the foundation of the world to be in God's plan, there was nothing he could do to get into it. This seemed to be so unfair. Then one day during Bible class, their pastor introduced him to another scripture he shall never forget. It is in Acts 13:48: "And when the Gentiles heard this, they were glad, and glorified the word of the Lord: and *as many as were ordained to eternal life believed.*" Of all the scriptures read that night, this one watered that seed that had been planted at his father's funeral, which he knew nothing about. After the Bible class that night, he asked Elder Walls if he could expound on this a little more for him. He said many believe something about God, but what these Gentiles believed was more specific. He said even the devil believed there was one God, but all he could do was tremble. He then told him to open his Bible and read Romans 10:8-14. He asked him if he understood what he had just read, and he told him he thought so; after all, he was a doctor. He then explained that he could not just have a head knowledge or understanding, but he needed to believe from his heart and believe something specific, that Jesus died only for those God elected. He instructed him to always pray before studying God's word so that God might open up his understanding to the scriptures, according to Luke 24:45. Then he instructed him to read John 17, the entire chapter. He said he and his wife, Sandy, would be praying for him. That night, he did what the pastor had suggested, and the spirit of God came over him. He was scared at first because he could hear himself speaking words but did not know what he was saying. He got his tape recorder out and recorded himself as this happened off and on for nearly an hour. When it was over, he was covered in sweat and water. That Sunday, he went to church and told his experience to Elder Walls and Sandy. They said he had been speaking in another language as the spirit of the Lord was commanding him. He asked Elder Walls and Sandy what would happen next. They asked him if he believed that Christ died for those that God had given him, and he told him yes. Sandy said that he now needed to be identified with Christ, a ceremony called baptism. She showed him scriptures in Acts where the apostles baptized men in Jesus's name, and that was what he needed to do. He was reluctant to do this, but when the morning service was nearing its end, the pastor gave an invitation for anyone who wanted to be baptized to come forward. His body was taking him to the altar, and he could not control it. While being baptized in Jesus's name, he started speaking in this language again and could feel the spirit of the Lord engulf him. He felt like he had been sealed in warm Vaseline. He still feels that sealant today.

"That's some story," comments Erica. "I must confess, I don't attended church and have a hard time believing God picks and chooses who will be 'saved' and the rest of humanity will perish."

In her mind, however, Dr. Myers is disappointed that Eric did not share any more about his childhood, and she is reluctant to force the issue.

George Lee then bust into the office with the same jubilance he left with. Dr. Myers tells Eric he must share more about his beliefs to her later.

"I hope I'm not interrupting anything?" asks George.

"Not at all, George," insists Dr. Myers.

"Listen, Eric," states George, while looking at Dr. Myers. "What do you say Erica flies back with us to Ann Arbor?"

"What do you mean fly back with you?" asks a surprised Dr. Myers.

"We flew down here yesterday in one of the company jets," explains Eric. "You might as well get used to George's driving, that is if it's all right with your boss."

Dr. Myers picks up the phone and explains George's proposal to David Veil. Seconds later, she hangs up and tells her new crewmates she can leave just as soon as she gets her computer and star charts together. She escorts them to the lobby and asks them to return their guest badges and wait there for her. She will have to stop by her house to get her things and will then drive them all to the airport.

As George and Eric sign out of the guest registry and return their badges to Ms. Devereaux, George asks Eric what he and Dr. Myers were talking about when he barged in. Eric tells him he was describing how God had saved him. "What scriptures did you give her because I know you did, brother?" asks George.

Eric reaches into his pocket and retrieves one of his church's business cards. "Here, I'll write them down for you, G. You can read them on the flight home."

"Very funny, my man," cites George.

"Isn't that what the autopilot is for?" insists Eric jokingly as he winks at Ms. Devereaux.

George taps Eric on the shoulder and starts to walk away from the receptionist's desk, pointing to Dr. Myers heading in their direction. Eric picks up his briefcase and follows him.

"My car's parked in the employee's parking lot. I'll pick you guys up out front," suggests Dr. Myers. "Bill Rodgers, David Veil, and General Westbrook will fly up to Michigan later this evening. They want to get a look at the spaceship before tomorrow night's launch. They will fly back to Houston in time to start monitoring and tracking our flight."

Dr. Myers drives her crewmates to her home and invites them in while she packs some clothes. In the short time they are there, Erica has managed to pack two suitcases filled with clothes, her computer, her doctor's kit, and a briefcase. She enters the living room where George and Eric are waiting. Out of courtesy, the men ask her if they can assist with her bags. Erica nonchalantly replies, "I have two bags in my bedroom if you don't mind, and my medical bag is in the kitchen." George and Eric grin as they bring the luggage from her bedroom and toward the front door. Erica looks at them and throws her hands in the air and cries, "What?" They just laugh and put her things in the car.

The drive to the airport is short. George directs her as to where she can park. "I'll file our flight plan and meet you on board," directs George. Eric and Erica go directly to the jet. Dr. Myers is impressed as she approaches the plane.

"Wow," she utters. "You guys certainly travel in style."

With pride, Eric insists, "Just wait 'til you see the *Argo Navis!*"

"The *Argo Navis?*" she asks.

"Yes, Erica," replies Eric as he opens the hatch to board the plane. "Our ship is named the *Argo Navis.* Do you know where we got that from?"

"If my memory serves me correctly, it's the ship Jason and his Argonauts used in their quest for the Golden Fleece." Erica then turns toward Eric and puts her hand on his arm prohibiting him for proceeding, "Who in the heck came up with that name?"

"It was George and I," replies Eric cautiously. "Why do you ask?"

"I love it," she says. Then offering her hand to Eric for his assistance in helping her onto the first step of the plane, she continues, "I'm really looking forward to being with you two." Eric and Erica get settled in their seats, having put their belongings away.

Moments later, George enters the aircraft. "Man, we have traveled here and there and . . ."

". . . Who knows where," interrupts Erica.

"Right, Doc, right" remarks George as he holds out his hand to slap Erica's. "Now button up your belts, boys and girls. We're out a here." George takes his seat in the cockpit, fires up the engines, and makes some final adjustments to the instruments. George puts his headphones on and moves the aircraft onto the runway. The tower clears him for takeoff, and George punches it.

DESTRUCTION EVERYWHERE

rofessor Mueller recklessly drives his black Mercedes Benz right up to the front door of Raymond Richards's home and abruptly stops. He quickly exits his vehicle proceeding to the house without closing the car door. He viciously pounds on Raymond's door. Within seconds, a weary and tired Richards opens the door, and Professor Mueller storms in before Raymond Richards could invite him in. "Thanks for coming so soon, Professor," stresses an unshaven Raymond Richards to his alleged partner.

"Raymond, you look horrible," observes Professor Mueller. "What's going on? I've been trying to reach you for the past twenty-four hours, and suddenly I get this frantic call to meet you at your home." Following Raymond into his study, Professor Mueller sits on a couch while Raymond Richards causally strolls to his desk. Professor Mueller once again demands, "What's going on?"

An extremely nervous Raymond Richards composes himself behind his desk and stares away from Professor Mueller as he begins to speak. "Yesterday evening, Professor, two detectives from the Ann Arbor police department paid Pat and I a visit. They showed us a picture of a man and asked if we recognized him. Pat saw the picture first and denied ever seeing the man. Then I was given the photograph and, and . . ."

"And what, Raymond?" asks Professor Mueller impatiently.

"It was Chuck Johnson, Professor. It was a photograph taken of Chuck Johnson from the city morgue. Chuck Johnson is dead, Professor. He apparently died after being struck by a car. Having no relatives to call upon, the police came to see me because his security badge to my company was found on his body."

"So this is what has you all traumatized? I didn't know you and Johnson were that close," implies Professor Mueller.

"We aren't, or shall I say we weren't, Professor. But that's not what has me in such a melancholy mood. They questioned Pat about her whereabouts Tuesday morning. They said a jogger got the license plate of a car speeding from the scene and later discovered Chuck's body. I was late meeting you at the restaurant that day because I took Pat's car to the shop to get an estimate, unaware of what had caused the damage." Then, looking directly at Professor Mueller, Richards continues, "The authorities traced the license plate to Pat's car. They arrested her on vehicular manslaughter charges. They think my wife killed Chuck Johnson!"

A stunned Professor Mueller questions, "And what does your wife have to say about all this?"

"Pat confessed to hitting something but thought it was an animal. She admits it might have been a bad decision not to check but had absolutely no idea it was a man, less known Chuck Johnson. At least that is what she told the authorities," explains Raymond Richards. "I expect her story will check out and she will be released later tonight."

"You sound as if you don't quite believe her."

"Pat knew Chuck Johnson, Professor. The two of us have talked about him before. She lied to the detectives about not knowing Chuck, and my gut instinct tells me she is lying about the accident too."

"So what are you going to do, Raymond?" asks Professor Mueller as he runs his hands through what little hair he has left.

"That's why I called you, Professor," answers a weary Raymond Richards. "I don't know what to do." After pausing a moment, Raymond Richards changes the subject. "How is the mission coming along? Is everything on for Friday night?"

Professor Mueller updates Mr. Richards on the events surrounding Friday night's launch of the *Argo Navis* and its crew. He glances at his watch and informs his associate that Eric and George should soon be back in town from their trip to Houston. Professor Mueller believes Raymond Richards is hearing him but is not listening. He is not sure if he told Raymond that General Westbrook knows about Chuck Johnson. Professor Mueller stands and approaches Raymond, who likewise stands. "I'm heading back to the hangar, Raymond. Take a shower and get some rest. I want you to be at the launch tomorrow night. Call me on my cell should you need me."

Raymond escorts Professor Mueller to the door and promises he will get into bed. After watching Professor Mueller drive away, Mr. Richards takes the professor's advice, taking a shower and going to bed.

General Westbrook walks out of his office to give Helen Hayes some final instructions before leaving for the day and will not be returning until Friday evening. He wants Helen to make sure David Veil and Bill Rogers will be meeting him at the airport for the trip to Ann Arbor, Michigan. The professional she is, Helen knows all too well her employer's desires and expectations. Helen Hayes is confident she will fulfill her duties and is anxious for General Westbrook to leave. Helen has been able to ascertain much of what has been kept secret at the Space Agency for the past few weeks and is literally dying to share it with Elizabeth Devereaux.

Twice now, Helen has attempted to contact Elizabeth, but to no avail. "Where is that child," Helen says to herself. Just as she decides to leave her desk and venture to the lobby, her phone rings. She checks its display and is elated to see the caller ID indicates it's the lobby. Quickly punching the speaker button, Helen shouts, "Hey girlfriend, where have you been?"

"Excuse me, Ms. Hayes! This is Karen. I'm returning your call. I noticed you've been ringing this extension."

"I'm sorry, Karen, I was hoping to speak to Elizabeth Devereaux," apologizes Helen.

"Ms. Devereaux has left for the day. May I be of some assistance?"

"No thank you, Karen. I'm sorry I bothered you."

"No bother at all, Ms. Hayes. Have a nice day," conveys Karen.

Helen's enthusiasm instantly turns into concerns in regard to her friend's absence. The opportunity to enlighten Elizabeth Devereaux regarding recent events at the Space Agency drastically diminishes. It's unusual for Elizabeth not to contact Helen, especially in case of an emergency.

Helen Hayes sits at her desk and decides to telephone Elizabeth at her apartment. She looks out of her office window and notices the skies are starting to get dark. Browsing the weather channel on her computer, she discovers a storm is heading their way. For a moment, Mother Nature has diverted her attention away from her friend. But the devoted friend that she is, Helen rests back in her chair, takes a deep breath, grabs her telephone, and dials Elizabeth's home phone.

After the phone rings three times and just as Helen Hayes prepares to leave Elizabeth Devereaux a voice message, a faint voice answers, "Hello."

"Elizabeth, it's Helen, baby. I missed you this afternoon."

An obviously shaken Elizabeth tearfully echoes, "Hey, Helen," before breaking down in tears.

"What's going on, baby?" asks a very concerned Helen. "Talk to me, girlfriend. You know I'm here for you."

Struggling to hold back her emotions, Elizabeth Devereaux softly utters, "Thanks for calling and checking up on me, Helen. I know I can depend on you. You are definitely my best and truest friend, and I love you for it."

"So what's going on with you, baby? How can I help you?"

"Right now I'm not sure if there is anything you can do. I got news at work this morning that my father has been in a serious car accident and is not expected to survive. I've made arrangements to go to Detroit . . . ," but before she can finish, Elizabeth breaks down crying again.

"I'm so sorry, Elizabeth. I feel so helpless. Please tell me what I can do to help you, baby," pleads Helen.

"Helen, do you know how to pray?" asks Elizabeth out of desperation.

Not having any real idea how to answer Elizabeth, Helen is bent on consoling her pain-stricken friend. "I believe all you have to do is talk to him, God, ya know. He hears everything and will hear you speaking or even thinking."

"So do you think you could talk to him on behalf of my father, Helen? I would really appreciate it," insists Elizabeth. "I have to get going, Helen. I'll call you when I get to Detroit and find out more. Don't forget to pray for us!" Elizabeth Devereaux hangs up the phone and attempts to compose herself enough to finish packing some clothes and head to the airport.

Helen looks toward the sky outside her office and asks God, if he exists, to spare the life of her best friend's father and also to ease Elizabeth's suffering. Knowing there is not much else she can do, Helen finishes her boss's business and prepares to go home early.

Erica Myers, Eric Miller, and George Lee have landed at RNR Industries. Erica insists they go directly to the hangar housing the *Argo Navis*. George and Eric chuckle as Erica realizes they too have the same aspirations. The trio disembark from the plane with their baggage. George checks in at the tower, and Eric takes an excited Erica Myers (pulling her two bags for her) to the hangar housing the spacecraft.

In front of a closed-door hangar, Eric Miller proudly proclaims, "Here we are, Erica, hangar 13. Are you ready for this?"

Tightly grabbing hold of Eric's arm, Erica pleads, "Will you just open the door?"

Eric notices that Dr. Myers has closed her eyes so he must guide her in the door. After entering the security code unlocking and opening the door, Eric gently guides Erica through the hangar's side door and places their luggage on the floor. He stands behind her and positions her between himself and the spacecraft. He passionately appeals for her to open her eyes and gaze upon the vehicle that will change the world. Opening her eyes, Erica Myers stares at the *Argo Navis* for a solid minute, shaking her head with her hands to her face and repeating, "This is unbelievable, truly unbelievable. It's a jet-black flying saucer!"

"Believe it, Doctor. Shall we go on board?"

"I might not want to leave," admits Dr. Myers.

"Let's hope you have that choice, Doctor. Let's go on board," invites Eric.

"Where is the entry hatch?" asks Erica Myers.

Eric smiles as he gives her a pair of gloves, "You're going to love this. Put on these gloves and follow me."

Dr. Myers reluctantly inserts her hands into the gloves, not knowing what significance this has in regard to her question. She follows Eric up a ramp but is unable to distinguish the front of the vessel from the back. Erica's eyes get wide and her mouth opens as she slows her pace noticing Eric appears to be walking right into the ship. Eric stretches forth his arm and suddenly disappears right into the ship. "Oh my God!" she shouts. Suddenly, she hears Eric's voice from within the vessel say, "Just extend your hand and follow my voice." Erica does as she is instructed, extending her arm and entering the ship, where Eric Miller patiently awaits.

"Welcome aboard the *Argo Navis*, Dr. Myers" Extending his elbow toward Dr. Myers, Eric continues, "Let me give you a tour of *our* vessel." Dr. Myers inserts her hand underneath Eric Miller's elbow and takes note that he called the vessel *ours*. Erica is without words as her gentleman friend begins the tour. She trusts he will also explain the magic door. "We have entered the ship on the starboard side. The hatch, as well as many other ship systems, is holographic. The gloves are used to activate the systems without having to touch them. To our left is the gallery and lounge, fully stocked for at least a month in space. Next to the gallery is a lavatory, the only one on the ship, if you get my drift. Next to the rest room is the ship's infirmary. Please feel free to make this your office and settle in as you please. George will get you setup with access code authentication and voice recognition. Moving on, we have the navigator's quarters, or shall I say your quarters, followed by the captain's quarters, or George's quarters. Now I take it you will recognize this section as the front of the ship or the bridge. Be careful Erica, this hatch in the middle of the floor leads to the lower engineering level or basement as we call it. To the right of the hatch is the navigator's chair and console. On the left is the captain/pilot's station. To his right is the copilot's chair and station, and below him is the engineer's chair and station. Outside the bridge is the copilot's quarters followed by the engineer's quarters. Last but not lease, we are back at the entry/exit hatch. What do you think thus far?"

"This is all so amazing, Eric. I never dreamed of such a thing. So what's in the engineering level or basement?" asks Dr. Myers.

"Well, Erica, while George designed and built this ship, the lower level we call the basement is where my hyperspace engine and the ship's power plant are housed." Eric moves to the front center of the ship and using his glove opens the basement hatch without bending over or coming into physical contact with it.

"I take it you are going to explain how this magic works, right?" asks Dr. Myers.

"Absolutely, Erica! Absolutely! Be careful as you step down the ladder. It's rather tight down there." Lowering themselves to the basement, Eric points out the forward and aft thrusters, the hydrogen and oxygen tanks, the bdellium energy cells, the matter and antimatter containment chambers feeding the reactor core, and the main engine thrusters taking up the entire center of the ship and exiting the rear. The engineering instrument consoles are presently cloaked.

"I know nothing about physics and propulsion, Eric," admits Dr. Myers. "My life is in your hands." Erica turns toward Eric and finds herself close to him. She feels comfortable and rests her hands on his chest. "I trust you and George and feel confident that you two scientists will see us safely through."

Putting his hands on Erica's waist, Eric feels her move even closer. "There's something about you, Erica. I just can't put my finger on it. Do you know what I mean?"

"I do, Eric, and I believe I know what it is," explains Erica.

Just as Eric waits for Erica to continue, they hear George yell, "Anyone on board?"

Eric takes a deep breath and pointing to the ladder suggests they return to the main level. George has with him Erica's personal belongings and is eager to get Erica setup and be familiar with the ship's consoles. He tells them that RNR Industries has provided food for them in the cafeteria and has hotel accommodations for Dr. Myers; however, Erica expresses an interest to spend the night on the ship. Erica gets her computer and asks George to show her how to interface it with the ship's computers. As George takes her to the navigation station, he turns to Eric and informs him that Professor Mueller was on his way to the hangar and wanted to speak to the three of them.

General Westbrook, David Veil, and Bill Rodgers have met one another at Houston's Hobby Airport and are preparing to leave on a private jet to Detroit. David Veil informs them that Erica has flown to Ann Arbor ahead of them with her shipmates. General Westbrook makes sure they understand that the trip to RNR Industries is to validate the authenticity of the mission, and they are returning to Houston that night. He informs David Veil and Bill Rodgers that a storm system is brewing in the Gulf, and he wants to be back at mission control well ahead of it, with plenty of time to track the spacecraft. Bill Rogers convinces General Westbrook that everything is all set, and mission control specialists have been briefed on their assignments. Both David Veil and Bill Rodgers are much more interested in viewing the vessel than tracking it. Upon arrival at Detroit's Metro Airport, they acquire a limousine and head for Ann Arbor.

Professor Mueller arrives at RNR Industries just ahead of the limousine carrying General Westbrook, David Veil, and Bill Rodgers. Professor Mueller greets his guests and takes them to the main conference room in the office building. After resting their belongings, they are anxious to see the spacecraft, and Professor

Mueller knows this. Professor Mueller pulls out his cell phone and calls Eric Miller. Eric tells him he and his shipmates are in the *Argo Navis* and were expecting him. Professor Mueller informs him their guests from Houston will accompany him to the hangar. They walk to hangar 13; Professor Mueller enters the security code and accesses the building.

Once inside, the delegation from the Space Agency finds George Lee, Eric Miller, and Dr. Erica Myers standing just a few feet from the ramp leading to the saucer's entry hatch. The entourage is visibly overwhelmed by the ship's size, shape, and color. Eric Miller asks Dr. Erica Myers if she wouldn't mind giving them a tour of the *Argo Navis*. George removes the cloaking protocols, allowing their guest to enter the ship without needing the gloves and to view the elaborate instrumentation consoles. Professor Mueller asks them to meet in the executive conference room after the tour, where he along with George Lee and Eric Miller will be waiting. On the way to the executive conference room, Professor Mueller informs Eric Miller and George Lee everything he knows about Chuck Johnson and his unfortunate demise. He also informs them of Raymond Richards and his wife Pat's involvement in the death of Chuck Johnson and Raymond's involvement with the NIA but is confident this will not affect the outcome of their mission. George Lee updates Professor Mueller that with the exception of completing the interface of Dr. Myers's computer with the *Argo Navis* navigation systems, the ship and crew are on schedule for Friday night's launch.

Moments later, an excited Dr. Erica Myers (escorted by the control tower chief) leads General Westbrook, David Veil, and Bill

Rodgers into the executive conference room. David Veil and Bill Rodgers walk straight to Eric Miller and George Lee and begin to bombard them with questions. General Westbrook corners Professor Mueller, expressing a concern that everyone involved be on the same page. Professor Mueller agrees and requests everyone's attention. General Westbrook also takes a stand next to Professor Mueller and demands everyone to move to the front of the room and take a seat.

"Let me first of all thank each of you for your contributions to this endeavor," insists General Westbrook. "I believe the union we have forged here this week and the vessel we intend to launch will usher this country into a new age and dimension of space exploration. Having said this, we need to be aware that there are principalities and powers that would foil our efforts and pervert this technology. Just recently, we were made aware of an NIA operative by the name of Chuck Johnson who infiltrated RNR Industries to gather information on this project. We are positive NIA director Walter Kennedy is behind this conspiracy but not sure how deep it runs and to what his final objective is. Finally, I am sad to notify you that local authorities discovered the body of Chuck Johnson, allegedly a victim of an unfortunate car accident. Professor Mueller, would you like to add anything?"

Professor Mueller motions for Eric Miller to join him at the podium and whispers something into his hear. And after receiving a positive nod for Eric, he addresses the audience. "You might notice that Raymond Richards is not with us today. Pat Richards, Raymond Richards's wife, is being held in connection with this tragedy, and there is nothing to suggest it was anything other than an accident. Raymond Richards is resting at home and is expected to be with us for tomorrow night's launch. Finally, there are details I won't get into right now, but some of us expect there might be another ship under construction. I think it's to our mutual advantage that we trust one another. That is why General Westbrook and I have shared this information with you and wish you well on your maiden voyage."

Elizabeth Devereaux exits the Jetway at Metropolitan Airport in Detroit. Her foremost thoughts are on her critically injured father. Elizabeth locates and follows the signs to the baggage claim area, where the single piece of luggage she brought with her awaits. After retrieving her bag, Elizabeth heads toward the taxicabs. The next available driver notices her approaching, drives up to meet her, and opens the trunk. Exiting his car, he walks around to where she is standing, opens the rear passenger's door, and remarks while reaching for her luggage, "Those wheels really come in handy huh! Where can I take you, ma'am?"

"My father lives in Detroit, but he is in a college hospital in Ann Arbor. How far is Ann Arbor from Detroit?"

"Well, miss, Ann Arbor is roughly twenty-five miles west of the airport and Detroit is east of here. There's about fifty miles between the two, depending on where in Detroit your father lives. Would you like me to take you to the college hospital?" asks the taxi driver.

Attempting to hold back the tears, Elizabeth Devereaux responds, "Yes, college hospital please."

The taxi driver is sensitive to his passenger's sorrow. "Not a problem, miss. You just sit back and try to relax. I'll have you there in no time." Several times, the taxi driver felt obliged to strike up a conversation, but his compassion overruled his curiosity.

Ms. Devereaux stares thoughtlessly out of the window during the entire journey, never once changing her posture. With only her father in her thoughts, it seem like mere seconds past between the time the taxi driver departed from the airport and the time he announced their arrival at the college hospital in Ann Arbor.

"I sincerely trust everything works out for the best for you and your family," states the taxi driver. "That'll be twenty bucks, miss." Looking into his rearview mirror at his passenger, the driver realizes she has not heard him. He turns in his seat, facing Ms. Devereaux, and repeats, "We have arrived at the college hospital in Ann Arbor. The fare comes to twenty dollars, miss." After pausing for a few seconds, he gently amplifies his voice and asks, "Are you going to be all right, miss?"

"Yes, of course. Thank you for asking. How much do I owe you, sir?"

"That'll be twenty dollars, ma'am."

Ms. Devereaux reaches in her purse and hands the taxi driver twenty-five dollars. He thanks her, exits his vehicle, and opens the door for her to exit. Extending his hand to Ms. Devereaux, the taxi driver assists her out of his cab. The driver then retrieves her luggage from the trunk. "I sincerely hope everything works out for you and your family, miss," reiterates the driver. "Take care!"

Ms. Devereaux slowly enters the hospital and walks to the main receptionist's desk. "Martin Devereaux's room please," she asks.

The receptionist enters the name into the computer. She then looks at Ms. Devereaux and asks if she is a family member. Fearing the worse, Elizabeth Devereaux nervously says yes, expecting the receptionist to give her some bad news. Instead, the receptionist writes down the room number on a card, hands it to her, and directs her to the elevators. Visiting hours on this floor are extended to family members of critically ill patients. Elizabeth's legs feel as if they have cement on them as she staggers to the elevators. Her body is draining its strength like a hole in a ball with every step she takes. She knows this is not good for her, but she does not know what to expect as she draws closer to her father's room. This was not the way she wanted to see him after so many years. The elevator door opens to a quiet intensive care unit. A sign posting room numbers and directions catches Elizabeth's eyes. To her surprise, her father's room is the first one past the nurses' station, not giving her much time to prepare for what awaits her. Elizabeth's heart pounds harder and harder. Just as she is about to enter into the room, she feels pressure on her arm. She looks over to see a nurse move in front of the door impeding her progress. The nurse very politely introduces herself and asks if she may assist her. Elizabeth takes a deep breath and introduces herself as Mr. Devereaux's daughter, Elizabeth. The nurse insists on briefing Elizabeth on her father's condition before she sees him. Elizabeth thanks her and then breaks down crying, dropping her luggage on the floor. A passionate and experienced nurse wraps her arms around Ms. Devereaux, practically carrying Elizabeth and her suitcase to the lounge.

"Is it that bad?" asks Elizabeth, feeling the chair under her as she slowly sits.

The nurse takes a deep breath and drops her head while grasping Elizabeth's hand and replying. "It's pretty bad, Elizabeth. We did not expect he would make it out of emergency. But he's a fighter."

"What did you say your name was again?" asks Elizabeth.

"I'm Helen," replies the nurse.

Looking directly into the nurse's eyes, Elizabeth admits, "My best friend's name is Helen." Now exhibiting signs of a smile for the first time today, Elizabeth acknowledges, "Thank you so much for being so kind to me, Helen. Can I ask you something?"

"Sure, Elizabeth, be my guest. I just hope I can give you an answer!"

"Do you know how to pray?"

"I think so," answers Helen. "Prayer is just talking to God. Everyone can talk to God; most folks just don't do it. There's a chapel on the second floor if you would like to pray or be alone. Would you like to go there first or are you ready to see your father?"

Taking a deep breath and taking hold of Helen's hand, Elizabeth replies, "I think I'd like to see my father."

"I won't lie to you, Elizabeth, your father's injuries are life threatening."

Elizabeth acknowledges the nurse by nodding her head. The two women slowly enter Martin Devereaux's room. The nurse pulls back his curtain and ushers Elizabeth forward. Martin's body is covered up to his neck, with his hands lying on top of the sheets and straight by his side. Tubes pumping fluids into his arms are connected to machines. His body moves in concert with the machines keeping him alive. The only exposed parts of his head are badly discolored, the rest covered in bandages. Elizabeth desperately fights back the tears as she touches her father's arm. The cool hard texture causes her to quickly retract her hand. Nurse Helen takes Elizabeth's hand and places it in her father's and does not allow her to let go until she feels comfortable grasping it alone. Nurse Helen pulls up a chair and assists Elizabeth into it before courteously leaving her alone. No sooner does Helen reach the door than she hears Elizabeth's deep sobs. She turns and notices Elizabeth's head buried into her father's bed, still grasping hold of his hand. Helen quietly closes the door behind her.

Half an hour later, a weary, tear-soaked, red-eyed Elizabeth staggers to the nurses' station. She asks Helen if she can direct her to the second-floor chapel. After giving Elizabeth directions, Helen offers her assistance, but Elizabeth politely declines.

Having been on her knees in the chapel for what seemed to be an eternity, and having drained nearly every drop of water from her body through tears, a solemn peace envelops Elizabeth and beacons her to return and stay at her father's side. She realizes that a portion of her strength has been renewed. A partially energized Ms. Devereaux boldly returns to her father's room. As midnight approaches, signaling the end of her shift, Helen returns to Martin Devereaux's room to find his daughter calmly by his side.

Nurse Helen quietly approaches Elizabeth and gently embraces her. "My shift is over soon, Ms. Devereaux. Can I get you anything, a blanket and a pillow maybe?"

"Yes, please," replies Elizabeth. "I want to thank you for suggesting I go to the chapel. I believe God has answered my prayers."

"A minister who comes here often to pray for the sick told me once that God hears everyone's prayer," admits Helen.

"So when we pray to God, he changes things, right?" insists Elizabeth.

"Deacon Miller is the minister's name," recalls Helen. "He says that when we pray, the thing that God changes is us! Good night, Ms. Devereaux, and good luck."

Embracing Nurse Helen, Elizabeth whispers, "I know I couldn't have made it today without you, Helen. Your compassion and godly insight have been encouraging. Good night." With that said, Elizabeth releases the nurse and returns to her father's side, eventually falling asleep in her chair.

General Westbrook, David Veil, and William Rodgers return to Houston just ahead of an approaching tropical storm. By Friday morning, they must make sure the old Apollo mission control center is ready to monitor one more flight.

George Lee, Eric Miller, and Erica Myers decide at midnight on the day before their maiden voyage that further preparation would not increase the chances of a successful mission but fatigue from working late hours could. George Lee has instructed his shipmates in every aspect of its operation. Dr. Erica Myers has successfully integrated her software navigation system into the guidance systems of the *Argo Navis*. Dr. Myers has suggested her shipmates get better acquainted with her and enjoy one last night out before becoming indefinitely confined together in deep space, possibly leaving this planet for good. George Lee would have them spend a few hours at a local pizza bar, while Dr. Myers would prefer to stay on the ship. However, Eric Miller's idea of ordering out and spending the night at his home took root and became a reality.

Eric has generously prepared his guests overnight accommodations. From carryout menus, they each order their favorite fast food. After eating what Eric deemed "the last supper," they sit around a lit fireplace in his den and discuss their past. Eric and Erica sit on Eric's large sofa directly in front of and parallel to the fireplace, while George sits on some pillows on the floor between them and the fire. George begins this conversation by admitting that throughout his life, he has lacked confidence with women. He believes a fear of rejection prohibits him from approaching and feeling comfortable around members of the opposite sex. He has no idea when this behavior started. George says he notices how confident and effortlessly this comes to Eric. Erica turns to Eric and asks if George's observation of him is valid. Eric, directing his attention to George, answers Erica's inquiry stating that God has given him the ability to fearlessly communicate with individuals regardless of race or sex. Eric concludes that he has always had this confidence. Erica picks up this thought and asks Eric to expound on his past, attempting to discover more about him. However, Eric turns the object of the conversation back to Erica and George by asking them both to make a statement concerning their mission. They both indicate that proving this vessel can sustain warp speeds and return home safely is all they hope for. On that note, the trio retires for the night.

Early Friday morning, General Westbrook instructs the flight directors as they prepare for the late night launch of the *Argo*

Navis. Eric Miller, George Lee, and Dr. Erica Myers arrive early at hangar 13 and board their spacecraft. All three put on their membrane gloves and start final preparations for their respective stations. George contacts mission control in Houston and verifies their ability to communicate as well as provide them with Dr. Myers's navigational vectors that will take them out of the solar system. Eric Miller and Professor Mueller have reviewed all antimatter propulsion protocols and are ready to start the engines of *Argo Navis.* The hangar crews move the *Argo Navis* outside the hangar for the first time. Erica Myers decided to leave the ship, attempting to contact her mother one last time before their departure. Raymond Richards arrives on site at RNR Industries in good spirits and updates Professor Mueller concerning his wife. After a few moments, Dr. Myers quietly returns to the *Argo Navis.* Eric and George concentrating on their respective tasks do not sense Erica's return or her troubled spirit. Raymond Richards and Professor Mueller board the spacecraft and give their young crew final instructions and encouragement. Mission control now starts a fifteen-hour count down to the after dark launch of the spacecraft. All communications between the Space Agency, the RNR Industries, and the astronauts have been verified.

Professor Mueller and Raymond Richards leave the ship and join the employees from EM Laboratories, Mueller Engineering, and RNR Industries at a safe distance from the ship.

George Lee and Dr. Erica Myers have secured themselves at the pilot and navigation stations, respectively. Eric Miller, in the basement, opens a ship-wide communications channel to George and Erica. "All systems online," states Eric.

"Affirmative," replies George securing the hatch. Looking over at Dr. Myers, George asks, "You ready, Doc?"

"Ready as I'll ever be," proclaims Dr. Myers.

With the *Argo Navis* power systems online, the first test of the spacecraft will be its ability to float independent of the docking platform. "Releasing docking clamps," replies George. The bottom side of the *Argo Navis* starts to glow as the antigravity systems are activated. This causes the ship to hover.

All of the bystanders are amazed at how steady the ship floats without a sound. George radios the tower and notifies them that the *Argo Navis* is moving to the launch site. Both the flight controllers at RNR Industries and the Space Agency acknowledge the saucers movement.

Eric transfers control of the engineering console to the bridge and starts up the ladder to the upper level. Looking back toward the engines, he pauses and whispers to himself, "God be with us." Entering the upper level of the ship, Eric locks the hatch and straps himself into the engineer's chair.

Glancing over his shoulder, George asks, "You ready, partner?"

"Let's do it, G," insists Eric. Checking his seating harness, Eric browses over at Erica Myers, "How about you, Doc? You ready?" Eric adjusting his vision notices what seem to be tears in Dr. Myers eyes. Instead of bringing this to everyone's attention, Eric extends his arm toward Erica. She extends her hand back to his and grasps it. They firmly hold each other's hands until Eric winks at Erica, and she breaks a smile.

The Space Agency announces, "T minus ten minutes and counting," David Veil, the flight director stands in the middle of row three of equipment in mission control. Bill Rodgers sits in the middle row and not only is monitoring the systems of the *Argo Navis* but also has additional responsibilities for the guys in the first row trench tracking the spacecraft. "*Argo Navis*, this is Bill Rodgers in systems. It's time for a final systems check."

"Copy that, systems director . . . ready when you are," replies George.

"Environmental systems, check?"

Pulling up that holographic system, George responds, "Environmental systems, check."

"Electrical systems, check?"

George looks at Eric who has that systems holograph open and throws the projection to George who acknowledges, "Electrical systems, check."

"Hyperdrive fuel and containment systems, check?"

Eric responds, "Hyperdrive fuel and containment systems, check"

"Guidance systems, check?"

George points to Dr. Myers to give a response who confidently acknowledges, "Guidance systems, check." George gives her a big thumbs-up as he continues to focus on the numerous indicators illuminated on nonholographic control panels.

"Hull integrity and inertia-dampening systems, check?"

"Hull integrity and inertia-dampening systems, check," acknowledges George.

"Communication systems, check?"

Looking sarcastically at Eric and Erica, "Communication systems, check."

"Verify time to launch at T minus five minutes and counting on my mark."

"Copy that, Houston. T minus five minutes on your mark."

George turns to Erica, "I see you have alpha-alpha entered into the computer."

"Absolutely, George. We'll launch with a rapid ascent and roll into a sustained high Earth orbit exactly one thousand miles above Earth. Should everything pan out, I have various beta routes mapped to test the warp drive. Then we can run the course you have plotted."

Suddenly, Erica and George look around to see Eric remove his safety harness and rush toward the basement hatch. Both George and Erica look as each other and wonder what could be so urgent to cause Eric to vacate his post literally seconds before the scheduled launch. Houston announces, "T minus two minutes and counting." A speechless Dr. Myers stares at George, anticipating he will take action. Seconds tick away, and Houston acknowledges, "T minus sixty seconds and counting." George squirms in his chair knowing that Eric is responsible for bringing the magnetic feed and nozzle systems online at T minus thirty seconds. George and Erica's hearts are pounding so hard you can practically feel their vibrations moving through their g-force chairs, and then the basement hatch opens and Eric emerges as if he were shot from cannon.

"T minus thirty seconds, *Argo Navis*, you are a go for magnetic feed and magnetic nozzle system activation," instructs Houston.

Quickly and without explanation, using his access gloves, George and Erica watch as Eric touches a series of instrument controls and practically out of breath replies, "Roger that, Houston, magnetic systems to thrusters online and ready."

The ship starts to shake slightly, then progressively more violently. "Don't worry, boys and girls, I expected this. It should soon subside. When it's time to launch, George, go easy on the throttle! Five to ten percent max, just like we planned," instructs Eric passionately. "Just like we planned, G!"

Taking a deep breath, George replies, "You got it, brother," securing himself for the launch. He takes his right hand and firmly grasps the thruster control.

Dr. Myers grasps her safety harness with her hands and pulls them close to her chest. "Strap yourself in, Mr. Miller?" she respectfully asks.

"Yes, thank you, Doc."

After a few long seconds, the spacecraft's vibrations taper off and subside.

Those on the ground at RNR Industries embrace one another. Grace says a silent prayer for her friends George, Eric, and their new partner Dr. Myers.

In Southfield, Pastor Walls senses a powerful urge to pray so he sets his Bible aside, goes to his wife in their the bedroom, holds her hand, and asks her to pray. Without question, she obeys.

"T minus ten, nine, eight, seven, six, five . . ."

"Diverting matter-antimatter stream from containment to magnetic feed systems," states Eric. "She's all yours, George."

"Four, three, two, one . . . *Argo Navis* you're clear for liftoff," declares Houston.

George looks back at Eric, who gives him a nod of approval. Then reciting the instructions Eric gave him in his mind, George slowly moves the throttle forward, absent of the ability to correlate the movement with their velocity.

A second seemed like eternity to the staff gathered outside hangar 13 as they hold their breath gazing at the black saucer hovering at the end of the main runway. Then in an unexpected blink of the eye, the *Argo Navis* whisks away into the dark, star-laden heavens on a beam of light. Another eternal second passes as those gathered realize the ship did not explode. Cheers erupt as the bystanders applause. Professor Mueller and Raymond Richards, however, race to the control tower where systems connected to Houston are set up to monitor the flight of the ship. Engineers in Houston are desperately attempting to locate the *Argo Navis*. It's not long before the enthusiastic crowd reenters hangar 13. It soon becomes apparent that Houston has a problem.

"Where's she at, David?" Bill Rodgers calmly asks. "She's out there somewhere, so somebody talk to me."

"She's definitely not on her scheduled flight path," replies Bill Rodgers. "We're attempting to track her warp signature from its origin. The good thing, I guess, is that we don't detect any debris, at least not within our present scanning range."

"That type of power could totally annihilate the vessel, could it not?" asks General Westbrook. "Are we certain this storm is not causing any interference?"

"The storm is definitely not having a problem on our systems, General," replies one of the engineers in the trench. "It might take us some time to recalibrate our sensors to detect the vessel's possible destruction, but I don't believe she blew!"

"Anything from NORAD?" calmly asks David Veil.

"NORAD is extending their range, but nothing on the radar," is the unidentified response from the trench. Also heard from the trench is the repeated message, "*Argo Navis*, this is Houston, please acknowledge."

Silence has overshadowed the employees at RNR Industries as they listen to the chatter in Houston, but none of them have left. Professor Mueller has noticed that the drama has taken Raymond's mind off the troubles with his wife.

"*Argo Navis*, this is Houston, please acknowledge."

"Where are we? What's happening? I feel a little light-headed. You guys okay?" asks Dr. Erica Myers.

"Yeah, Doc, I'm good," replies George after taking a deep breath.

"Yeah, yeah, I'm all right, Doc. I feel a little wheezy too," explains Eric.

"I'm opening the viewing portal," says George. "Let's get a look outside."

"There's nothing out there, George!" cries Erica. "No Earth, no moon, no nothing, just a lot of stars. Are we even moving, Eric? Where the heck are we?"

George with his eyes wide open reminds Erica that as the navigator, it is her job to determine their location as all three of them start running diagnostics on their respective systems. After a few moments of silence, George and Eric hear Dr. Myers repeat to herself that this can't be right. After about the third or fourth time, George asks, "What can't be right, Doc?"

"According to my calculations," she adds, "we did not follow the course I laid out. It seems as if we're mere minutes shy of Venus. Can you confirm this, Eric?"

"That's affirmative, Dr. Myers! It seems we have attained a speed of over fifty thousand miles per second." Constantly working his control panel, he says, "If my calculations are correct, we've sustained this speed for at least the last five or six minutes. If you check the navigation programming, Doc, the alpha-alpha protocols are in effect. Due to the high speed velocities, the ship was unable to perform your near-Earth maneuvers and executed the alpha-alpha instructions to set the vessel on a safe course through the solar system."

"So much for the spiral Earth orbit, Doc!" replies George in a joking manner.

Erica calmly looks over at George and responds, "That appears to be correct. If we are indeed moving, I don't feel a thing, not even on liftoff. The engines and the ship are really performing great," observes Dr. Myers, calming herself and the crew.

Eric concurs, "I agree, Dr. Myers. Engineering systems are running smooth. But I got a strange feeling something's not quite right. I can't put my finger on it, but something's wrong," contends Eric. "Listen, did you hear that?"

"Hear what, Eric?" asks Dr. Myers.

"I'm not sure, but it's very faint."

"Where is it coming from, the engines, the structural integrity? Can you be a bit more specific?" asks George.

"No, no, it's not the ship. I believe the ship is fine, George," suggests Eric. "Divert some of the reserve power from containment and apply it to communications. Boost the hyperspace radio antenna, George."

"You got it, brother," acknowledges George. "Let's see if there is some subspace shatter out there."

"You can do that, George?" asks Erica.

"I can try, Doc. I can try," repeats George as he tweaks the communications array.

George, Eric, and Erica become motionless and turn their ears toward the ship's communications speakers, like turning their heads will help. They wait for minutes hearing nothing more than the subtle hum of the warp-drive engines. Then unexpectedly they hear, "*Argo Navis*, this is Houston, please acknowledge."

The *Argo Navis* crew smile at one another in relief. They are not alone and have definitely accomplished what was the first and most important step of their mission. George prepares to open the communications channel and asks Dr. Myers if she would do the honors of replying to her coworkers. He tosses the holographic communications control panel to her to initiate the response. Looking at George before making her statement, she reminds both George and Eric that they are her shipmates and her friends.

"Houston, this is Dr. Erica Myers acknowledging from the spaceship *Argo Navis*, please continue," replies a very happy and energetic Erica Myers.

Everyone at the Space Agency goes wild with excitement, as does everyone at hangar 13 in Ann Arbor after hearing Dr. Myers's voice. People at both locations embrace one another and shout for joy. Some, including Grace in Ann Arbor, cry and praise God for sparing their companions.

"*Argo Navis*, this is Houston, you had us scared there for a moment. What's your twenty?"

"At best guest, Houston, we are closing fast on Venus."

"Venus!" shouts the flight director. Looking around, David Veil notices the excited engineers staring at him. "That's incredible. *Argo Navis*, what's your plan?"

"We'll, uh, have to get back to you on that one, Houston," replies Dr. Myers. "Are you tracking us?"

David Veil looks toward the engineers sitting in the trenches and asks them why they can't view the ship yet while pointing to the visual tracking board above their heads. Just before giving Dr. Myers and the *Argo Navis* crew a negative response, one of the engineers says that his systems were focusing on a smaller region of space around Earth. Because of the vessel's speed, he is widening the field of view. Immediately, the tracking board lights up, detailing Earth as the point of origin with the spacecraft rapidly approaching Venus.

"No problem, *Argo Navis*, but it would help if we could input your course correction and know where you're going," requests the flight director.

"Affirmative, Houston. We'll have to get back to you on that," repeats Dr. Myers. "Give us one minute, Houston."

Temporarily muting communications with Houston, Dr. Myers explains to the crew, "Look, guys, the ship has no real course. I'm going to start my first program that will leave the solar system entirely. It's clear sailing, no asteroid belt, no other planets, just open space," explains Dr. Myers. "Do you guys have any objections?"

"I want to test the engines at full throttle for an extended period, Dr. Myers. But I feel something is wrong with your first course," cautiously petitions Eric.

George does not totally agree with Eric. He would like to make sure the ship is structurally sound, but it makes no difference to him where they will go, as long as they go fast. With a two-to-one vote, Dr. Myers informs Houston that she is going to execute the first program in the flight plan she gave them, but Eric shakes his head in disagreement while not making a vocal comment. Houston acknowledges and prepares to track the vessel using on an ultrawide visual telemetry setting.

"Warning, warning, proximity alert, warning *Argo Navis*, proximity alert."

George quickly turns around in his chair and checks his instruments. "Approaching Venus, guys," he shouts. "I suggest before we execute your program, Doc, we slow down and establish a HALO around Venus. Please relinquish computer navigational control, Doctor."

"What the heck is a HALO?" she asks.

"High altitude orbit," George replies.

"Navigational control transferred to pilot," replies Erica. "You now have manual control, George. Do you copy this maneuver, Houston?"

"Affirmative, *Argo Navis*. We confirm you established a HALO around Venus."

Eric and Erica unbuckle and walk over to the large forward viewing portal to get a bird's eye view of Venus, the first human eyes to do so.

Dr. Myers whispers that never in a million years could she have dreamed of seeing a planet like Earth or Venus from space. What will I have seen after tomorrow. George momentarily joins them but returns to his station after a few moments. Erica Myers and Eric Miller likewise return to their stations and duties.

"Sending updated course corrections and flight plan, Houston," declares Erica.

Houston uploads the *Argo Navis* flight plan into their computers. David Veil explains that a hurricane has formed in the Gulf and is expecting to hit shore in about an hour. The flight director encourages the *Argo Navis* crew to continue communications; however, there could be intermittent signal loss or interruptions indefinitely, but he assures the crew they will be monitored and tracked.

George returns the ship to computer navigation before joining Eric and Erica in the lounge for a mission update. Dr. Myers goes through the galley and retrieves nutrition bars and energy drinks for herself and distributes one to each of her shipmates. After a moment of silence, she asks Eric Miller if there is something he wanted to share with them regarding execution of her first program, as he disagreed with it. He also seemed concerned that the ship executed the alpha-alpha instructions overriding her near-Earth maneuvers.

If he has some concerns about her programs jeopardizing the mission, she definitely wanted to hear them.

"It's not the mission, Doctor, and I assure both of you it's not either of you. I've got this awful feeling in my spirit that I can't explain. I don't mean to attack you, Erica, but I sense my feelings are linked to your flight plans. I'm sorry if that makes you uncomfortable, but you asked."

"Thanks for being honest with me, Eric. I was beginning to wonder. As a doctor, I need to constantly monitor our state of mind. We have been lucky thus far, and I would like to keep it that way."

"Not luck, Doc, we have been blessed. God has truly blessed us," explains Eric.

"You've been quiet, George. What's on your mind?" asks Dr. Myers.

George taking a sip from the beverage pack replies, "I don't know about you two, but after the brief nausea I experienced, I somehow feel great, really great. I am anxious to know what heading you gave Houston."

"Eric, why did you name the ship the *Argo Navis?*" asks Erica Myers.

"Are you familiar with Greek mythology, Erica?" he asks.

"Yes, I am," she replies. "It was one of my favorite topics in college. As an astronomer, the two subjects seemed to go hand in hand."

"Then you know the story of Jason and the Argonauts and their quest for the Golden Fleece."

"Yes, Eric, I'm familiar with that tale."

"Well, I'm not," interrupts George. "You said you were going to tell me the tale, Eric, remember?"

"Basically, George, the ship that carried Jason and his crew was called the Argo," explains Eric. "And collectively they were known as the Argonauts."

"I think you told me that much, my man, but why do I feel there is more?"

"Yeah, Eric, tell us why you gave *our* ship this name. Especially since the mission Jason's evil uncle sent him on was supposedly so dangerous he was certain not to return alive!" interjects Erica.

"Eric, tell me this is not so . . . !" insists a stunned George.

"Don't get uptight, G. Dr. Myers just wants to create some excitement around here. The master shipbuilder, Argo, for whom the ship was named, constructed the fifty-oared ship from the finest lumber in the land. And I might add, it was the largest ever built at that time," reassures Eric. "Oh yeah, the Argo's crew was a who's who of great warriors, the bravest adventurers from the most prestigious households in Greece."

"I feel a little better now, brother. But now I'm still curious, Dr. Myers, what's the name of the ship have to do with the course you gave Houston!"

"Well, George," starts an excited Dr. Myers, "one thing you will learn about me is that I am very much into the mythology surrounding the stars. To make a long story short, I have plotted a course toward the constellation Cygnus. It's far enough away. We could travel at high warp for years and not encounter any obstacles."

"So I take it there's a story here as well?" asks George.

Looking in Eric's direction, Erica answers, "It's a love story, George."

Eric smiles back at Erica. George responds as he leaves the lounge that he can't wait to hear this story. Eric and Erica finish their beverage with Erica returning to her console and Eric stopping at his engineering station just long enough to grab his gloves and go into the basement.

Fifteen minutes later, Eric returns to his engineering station on the bridge, informs his shipmates that his check of the engines are complete, and he is ready to break orbit about Venus and head for Cygnus. Seconds later, the trio secure themselves, and George launches the spacecraft into hyperspace.

Sometime in the early morning hours, Martin Devereaux passes away. Elizabeth Devereaux is so thankful she was able to be by his side at the end. Nurse Helen offers to drive Elizabeth to the home of Martin Devereaux in Detroit. Elizabeth is eager to discover as much as possible about her father's last few days. She has never been to her father's home, and upon arrival, she collects the mail that has accumulated since her father's accident. She discovers a traffic citation from the Detroit police department. The citation reveals that her father was responsible for the accident that led to his death. Nurse Helen watches a television news program while giving her new acquaintance time to reflect. Elizabeth joins the nurse and sits with her. The two comment on the weather that is destroying property in Texas, the home state of Ms. Devereaux. Elizabeth turns to Helen and comments that destruction seems to be everywhere. She further indicates that it's time to start making final arrangements for her father and would like to be alone. Before leaving, Helen offers her condolences for the passing away of Elizabeth's father and was glad Elizabeth was there at his side. The two women embrace before Helen leaves Elizabeth to mourn. Elizabeth closed the door and begins to cry.

As the *Argo Navis* races out of the solar system, the feelings agonizing Eric Miller's spirit return. He retreats to his quarters to pray in private; however, his unrecognizable language could not be muffled. After about an hour, a concerned Dr. Myers asked Eric Miller if everything was all right. A teary, red-eyed Eric emerges from his quarters, shaking his head, indicating the opposite. Eric immediately and urgently requests that George stop the vessel. A surprised George, thinking Eric is joking, just smiles without turning to facing him. Eric touches George on the shoulder and pleads for George to turn the vessel around.

Turning in his chair, George answers, "What's going on, Eric? You're serious, aren't you?"

"Eric, sit down a moment and talk to me," asks Dr. Myers. "What's this all about? Does this have anything to do with why you left the bridge before liftoff?"

"Before liftoff was something else. I'm not sure what this is," replies Eric wiping his eyes. "All I'm sure of is that I have a very strong sense that destruction is all around us."

George shouts, "Is there something wrong with the ship or the engines, Eric?"

"No, no, G, the ship is fine," assures Eric.

George looks at Dr. Myers, "Doc!"

"Eric, come with me to the lounge," demands Dr. Myers. Then looking at George, she insists, "I'll find out what's going on, but do not stop the ship!"

After over an hour with Eric, Dr. Myers exits the lounge and sits hard in her chair. "How well do you know Eric?" she asks of George. "Mentally, I mean."

"Is he losing it, Doc? Is space affecting him? Could I be next?"

"Just answer the question, George. Do you believe Eric to be stable mentally?"

"Yes, of course, Dr. Myers. If someone was to lose it on this trip, I would have thought it would be me," asserts George.

"I'm going to give Eric a sedative so he can rest. I suggest we all get some sleep. Doctor's orders, George."

George closes down his station and assists Dr. Myers with Eric before retiring to his quarters. Dr. Myers wants them to get at least eight hours of sleep. She has second thoughts about informing Houston of their situation. Hypertravel delays the signal reaching Earth, and she hopes that the issues will subside with rest. She does, nevertheless, make a journal entry in her personal log, noting that without any substantial evidence, Eric Miller seems stressed about continuing on this present course. She also notes that she believes the name of the ship might have some psychological bearing on Eric Millers mental state.

Inconspicuously getting the flight director's attention, one of the engineers monitoring the trajectory and flight of the spacecraft whispers to David Veil that there is something he should see. He nervously points to a large, dark, and rapidly growing phenomena, totally absence of stars, and headed right for Earth. He further explains that it seems to be emanating from the last known position of the *Argo Navis*. David Veil asks if there was an equipment malfunction for which the engineer emphatically denied. General Westbrook joins them just as the engineer confirms NORAD and other deep space monitoring agencies are reporting the same occurrences. Before General Westbrook could ask, the engineer looks at him and adds that NORAD estimates the anomaly will overtake the planet in roughly nine hours.

"Get me the president, son," orders General Westbrook.

BELIEF IS IN YOUR HEART

Eric Miller awakens after only four hours of rest. He checks on his shipmates who appear to be sound asleep. While they slept, Eric sought after and pilfered a vial of ether he discovered in Dr. Erica Myers's medicine kit, unaware she knows of his presence in her quarters. His intentions are to render his crewmates unconscious while he plots a course back to Earth. Opening the vial and pouring the solution into a cloth, he approaches Dr. Myers. Lying on her side with her back to him, Dr. Erica Myers remains motionless, wondering to what extent Eric Miller will carry out his plan. She feels him kneel down behind her. The second she feels he is about to subdue her, preparing to defend herself, he stands and takes a step backward. Sensing Eric has aborted or postponed his plan, she continues to lie still. Quietly, Eric Miller exits Dr. Erica Myers's quarters. Dr. Myers takes a deep breath, contemplating how she will handle this. Slowly turning her head and looking back, she notices he has left the vial of ether and cloth. Now sitting at his engineering station on the bridge, Eric Miller realizes they are still on course to Cygnus and immediately drops to his knees and begins to pray.

"Hallelujah, vo-ithia emena Jesus, thank you, Lord. Ego khriazomeh esi Theos," cries Eric softly, but audible enough to be heard.

From her quarters, Dr. Myers listens. Her curiosity takes her to the bridge. While sitting at her navigation station, Erica notes the atmosphere feels as if there is a third presence with them. She looks around to see if George has joined them, but no one else is there. Eric's chants get louder, but not to the point of awakening George.

"*Emis khriazomeh esi oh Theos, vo-ithia emena, vo-ithia emena hallelujah. I love you, Lord. Thank you, Jesus*," cries Eric. "Thank you, Lord, oh God. We need you."

As Eric calmly ceases to pray, it takes him a few seconds to realize that Dr. Myers is sitting with him. He rises and sits in the engineer's chair. "Dr. Myers, I'm sorry if I disturbed you."

"That's all right, Eric. I wasn't actually sleeping." Erica moves toward Eric and positions herself in front of Eric where he has kneeled. "Your prayers touched me. I felt a presence with us. I've never witnessed someone pray like that before. Why, may I ask, do you sometimes speak in a foreign language?"

"When the spirit of the Lord comes over me, I do not know what tongue I am speaking in," explains Eric.

"I've heard that some Christians speak in tongues. I believe that's what they call it."

"You are correct, Doctor. Nevertheless, I apologize if I disturbed you."

"In a way, I should be thanking you," confesses Dr. Myers.

"I'm sorry," admits Eric, "Why should you be thanking me?"

"I should be thanking you for not killing me," exhorts Dr. Erica Myers. She reaches into her pocket and exhibits a sealed pouch containing a cloth soaked with ether. "You put enough ether on this cloth to kill me, Eric. I knew you were in my quarters. I wasn't asleep. Will you please explain to me again what danger exists to the extent you would harm me and abort our mission?"

Eric lowers his head and embraces Erica. "I am so sorry, Dr. Myers. I could never harm you. You must believe that," admits Eric. He then confides once again his concern for continuing forward, this time in more detail. However, in light of the fact that all ship functions appear to be running smoothly, and this by Eric's own admission, Dr. Myers is still not convinced there is some unseen imminent danger.

Having programmed the ship to perform various maneuvers to test its agility, handling, and responsiveness and to test the engines, Dr. Myers asks, "Eric, if you have issues with my navigation, just let me know."

Assuming a kneeling position on the deck alongside Dr. Myers, Eric concludes, "It is actually your abilities to navigate hyperspace that I'm trusting in. I believe you have abilities you might not be totally aware of, abilities that could ultimately save mankind."

Eric Miller believes if he is going to persuade Dr. Erica Myers before it's too late, he must find some common denominator with which to reference. The spirit of the Lord leads him to use her navigational program as a point of reference. He asks Dr. Myers if rhetorically she could explain how her navigational programming was able to intuitively adapt and execute the alpha-alpha course corrections when the increased velocity of the vessel rendered its original flight plan useless as they launched. Dr. Myers replies to him that she really has not thought about that. He then explains to her that the failsafe protocols she intuitively programmed into her courses are part of her natural instincts to recognize danger and seek the best possible resolution. Conscious that Dr. Myers is preparing to stand, Eric Miller assists her and while doing so inconspicuously touches her crippled leg, praying that God instantaneously heals it.

Returning to her navigational station, Dr. Myers slips on her gloves, pulls up her navigational console, and motions for Eric to come closer. Opening her navigational program code, she points to a subroutine she wrote years ago to interface with a vessel's computers. She created algorithms that went out and plotted courses relative to the vessel's current speed and acceleration. This subroutine runs continually, always checking current speed versus current course, and makes the necessary corrections. Her belief and thinking at the time was in expectation that computers would be sophisticated enough to integrate navigational systems, with engines and guidance systems, and determine when the present course settings are inappropriate. She did not remember these routines were there. Dr. Myers admits that she was just playing around with some thoughts at the time and didn't realize these subroutines were still in the system and glad she didn't delete them. Dr. Myers surmises that since her earlier programming could not account for the speed, weight, and other necessary variables of *Argo Navis*, it thought to look for a course that did. It discovered the alpha-alpha course and engaged it. "I thank God they were there," she adds. "Are these the sort of abilities you are referencing?"

"Yes, my friend, and even more," suggests Eric. "So what do your instincts tell you about Cygnus and any significance in going there?"

"So who's the doctor now?" asks Erica as she turns and faces Eric. "To tell you the truth, Eric, I have always been fascinated with the story surrounding the star more than the star. But why do you ask?"

"I believe with all my heart that the two of us have much in common," explains Eric. In her mind Erica thinks, *If he only knew.* "I also believe that if I can find some common point of reference between us, you will understand why I am so animate about reversing our course."

Dr. Myers agrees, "All right, Eric Miller, I'll buy that. But let me ask you this, are you just curious about why I chose Cygnus, or might this have something to do with finding our common ground?"

"Actually, I'm hoping a little of both," replies Eric with a smile.

"Fair enough, Eric Miller," says Dr. Erica Myers. "One of the stories surrounding the constellation Cygnus involved two friends, Phaethon and his friend Cygnus. Phaethon was born from a brief liaison between the sun god Helios and the nymph Clymene. When Phaethon reached manhood, he discovered his father's true identity, that of a god. With his friend Cygnus, Phaethon sought out Helios and demanded that he drive the chariot that the sun god used to carry the rays of the sun across the sky. Helios gave into his son's demands. Phaethon had no experience driving a chariot with this much power and soon started driving recklessly. Zeus intervened and hurled a thunderbolt at the chariot, and Phaethon fell into the Eridanus River. Cygnus then dived into the river to search for this friend's body. After numerous attempts, Cygnus eventually died from exhaustion, and Zeus again intervened by turning Cygnus into a swan so he could continue to search for Phaethon. To this day, Cygnus looks for his friend." Tears start to come from Erica's eyes, so she went to her quarters to dry her face.

George Lee passes her on his way to join them on the bridge. When he sees Eric, he comments, "I don't know what it is about you, but you seem to break more hearts!"

"It's not like that at all, G," explains Eric. "Erica was explaining to me why she chose the constellation Cygnus as our targeted destination. I needed to find some common reference point to prove to her, and you, why we need to abort this present course."

"No problem man, I know nothing about mythology, nor do I really care to. You guys go right ahead. I know she told me you have your concerns. But she's the doc. She'll hook you up."

"George!" shouts Eric softly.

"Or maybe not," reverses George. "Hey, man, ya know what, I feel great. By the way, did you notice that Dr. Myers was no longer limping?"

As Erica returns from her quarters, Eric looks at her and replies to George, "You're right, G. She's not limping anymore!"

"You all right, Erica?" asks Eric.

"Yes, Eric, I'll be fine," she assures him.

"Please continue if you don't mind," says Eric. "This is getting interesting."

Erica takes a deep breath and wipes her nose. "You see, Eric, I can really relate to Cygnus and the friendship he had with Phaethon. As another myth puts it, Cygnus might have had some kind of birth defect. He was set out on the seashore to die. However, a swan took pity on him and flew down to care for the newborn. I really sympathize with Cygnus. Swans occur throughout the myths as gods transforming themselves into swans to seduce attractive nymphs."

"I can see how you can relate to Cygnus, seeing both of you had birth defects."

"Yes, Eric, but it's deeper than that. You see, when I was in elementary school, I had this friend that overlooked my handicap. In the eighteen months or so that I knew him, we became close. But one day, I missed him and found out that his family had moved away. Like Cygnus, I vowed to keep searching for this friend. Hopefully, you can understand my obsession with this constellation. I guess in my subconscious mind I programmed this course into my navigational system to remind me of this search."

"Don't you see, Dr. Myers, we both have something in common with this constellation," explains a rejuvenated Eric Miller. "Just think back on the reason Zeus threw the thunderbolt at Phaethon and my reason for wanting to discontinue our present course. Zeus felt Phaethon's reckless driving would destroy Earth. Our beliefs stem deep within our hearts."

"Okay, Eric Miller, but your beliefs are spiritually based. How do you relate that to Cygnus?" asks Dr. Myers.

"I too know something about this constellation, Erica Myers. It is also known as the Northern Cross," explains Eric. "Talking about spirituality, Cygnus with its long neck stretched out actually flies south for the winter. Around Christmas Eve at sunset, the cross stands upright on the northwest horizon."

"That's true, Eric, and brilliant," admits Dr. Myers. "You know if there was anything else, I might just reconsider making that course change."

"Then consider this," resumes Eric. "A small yet massive object orbits a giant star near the center of Cygnus known as Cygnus X-1. Most astronomers believe that Cygnus X-1 is a black hole!"

Dr. Erica Myers turns to George and politely informs him she will be disengaging her navigational program and allowing for manual control. Interrupting her, Eric says he believes they can travel anywhere in the universe, just not toward Cygnus. The vessel is performing flawlessly and they should continue testing it as well as some of Dr. Myers navigational programming. Dr. Myers assures Eric Miller that she has only removed the course to Cygnus from her programming and will update her report to the Space Agency, suggesting they never plot these coordinates in any hyper-driven spacecraft.

"I thank God for you both, and I am sorry for any pain I might have caused you," says Eric. He then turns and directs his attention to Erica. "Just because Cygnus never found his friend does not mean you will not find yours. Somewhere in Minnesota lies your answer."

"Minnesota, Eric?" asks Erica.

"Yes, Minnesota. Did you not tell us you moved to Texas from Minnesota?" asks a now bewildered Eric Miller. "I just thought your childhood friend might still be in the state where you grew up."

"Well, Eric Miller, first of all, I think I might have found him," suggests Dr. Erica Myers. "Second of all, I grew up in . . ."

Just then, the ship starts to shake as an airplane experiencing turbulence.

Eric jumps up and starts to open the hatch to the lower level. "I'll be in the basement. Use the ship's communications systems to stay in contact with me."

"You got it, brother," insists George.

George Lee and Dr. Erica Myers strap into their seats and frantically checks their respective systems. The *Argo Navis* still shakes as she moves through space at light speed. George contacts Eric and asks him if he thinks they should slow to sublight speed. Eric replies to give him a few seconds. He thinks he might know what the problem is. Dr. Myers firmly grips her chair. George consoles Erica that the ship is structurally sound. Inertia-dampening systems, guidance systems, and computers all check out. Dr. Myers confirms that her navigational computers are online, functioning within normal parameters and could not be causing this phenomenon. George suggests they wait for Eric's assessment, and Dr. Myers agrees.

"Try not to be nervous, Doc," encourages George. "As a test pilot, I've felt this kind of disturbance many times before. Granted we are a long way from home, I believe in this ship and its crew. We'll be just fine, you'll see."

"Thanks, George, I really needed that," admits Erica. "So you think Eric will find the problem?"

Before George could answer Dr. Myers, the *Argo Navis* stops shaking. Dr. Myers cautiously releases her hold on her seat.

"Eric's got her fixed!" shouts George in jubilation. "I told you he'd fix it, Doc."

"I'm interested in knowing what the problem was," questions Dr. Myers. This is the second time now Mr. Miller has retreated to the basement."

George, surprised by Dr. Myers's statement, jokingly responds, "Are you accusing Eric of intentionally sabotaging the ship, Doc?"

"Eric never told us what happened during our launch. Don't get me wrong, George," pleads Dr. Myers. "I trust both of you. I'd just like to know what went wrong."

"Why, did something have to go wrong?" asks Eric as he returns to the bridge. "I'm sorry for my preoccupation the past few hours, but I assure you both I have not lost sight of why we are here." Taking a seat at his engineering station, Eric puts on his gloves; and moving his fingers in the proper sequence, he activates the antimatter containment system, oblivious to Dr. Myers initial inquiry. "Take a look at this, boys and girls. I have been monitoring two systems, containment and energy management. When the amount of energy produced by the matter-antimatter explosions exceeds the amount required by the engines, the residual energy gets dumped to the containment system. The containment systems are basically massive energy-absorbing batteries. When the containment systems become saturated, either the energy requirements by the engines need to be increased by increasing our speed or the antimatter systems need to be shut down. I introduced a third alternative. I've been running a program that takes the saturation point energy from containment, adds that to the amount needed to sustain our present speed, and reduces matter-antimatter production. The problem here is that these systems are tied into our navigational system. When we briefly disengaged auto navigation and went on manual pilot, these systems did not convert over. I have thus rectified this problem by including manual control in the program's matrix."

"That explains the vibrations," adds George. "The two systems attempting to compensate had a lag time that resulted in inconsistent velocity vectors. Sort of like the points not firing on older model cars. Could an increase in speed have resolved this problem?"

"Yes, but it could have created a need for more power if the acceleration was not totally parallel with the excess energy," explains Eric.

"I'm curious, Eric?" asks Dr. Myers. "Why did you go into the basement just before liftoff?"

"I was wondering when someone was going to ask me that. You might not be aware, Erica, of the problem we had with inferior and duplicate parts. I walked away from this project when I suspected Professor Mueller or RNR Industries might have been involved with faulty components being substituted in place of the ones my company had manufactured. To make a long story short, when I replaced the noncompliant injectors, I left the electronic locking caps on, just like on the original parts and schematics. The thing I never got around to doing was creating an electronic control connector to a console, mainly the engineer's console, to manually disable the locking caps. With the locking caps engaged, we would have fried just seconds after engaging the antimatter drive. In the excitement, I failed to give you both an explanation, I'm sorry."

"I did not know the injectors had locking caps, lest known the fact that they could be enabled or disabled," cited George.

"I never documented it, G, not even on the schematics of the injectors," admits Eric. "You and Erica are the only ones, other than myself, that have this knowledge."

"Wow, secret injectors, Erica healed, what's next?" asks George.

Dr. Myers leaps out of her seat and slowly walks around the bridge while Eric and George silently look on. Trying to keep from shouting and remaining composed, Erica can hardly believe what has happened to her. She had no idea her limp was gone.

"When did you guys notice this?" she asks. "All my life I dreamed of being whole. Oh my God, this is amazing. Oh my God, please let this be permanent."

Dr. Myers returns to her seat and puts her hands over her face and cries. Eric and George both give her some space before Eric goes over to her. Resting his hand on her shoulder, he says he didn't notice it until George brought it to his attention as she was returning from her quarters.

Looking toward George, Eric asks him how his arm feels, the one he broke years ago that bothers him constantly. George replies that it is still bothering him but does not know what that has to do with Dr. Myers's leg. Eric continues by telling him there are those in the physical sciences community who theorize the energies produced from warp fields have some regenerating effects. "I have been keeping a personal log of how my knee feels, especially considering the amount of time I spend around the engines. My knee still hurts. The bottom line is that I do not believe there are any residual or miracle effects of warp travel or warp fields on our bodies."

A confused George then asks, "So what is your theory concerning Dr. Myers's leg? It would appear as if your deductions are wrong."

"I believe in the power of prayer, George. I prayed to God to heal her leg, and he did," replies Eric. "I also prayed he give you the confidence to see us through this mission."

Satisfied with Eric Miller's explanation, the trio return to monitoring their respective systems. Then George Lee turns to Dr. Erica Myers, remembering she was about to mention where she grew up before the issues with the locking caps arose. "Dr. Myers, you were about to tell us before the turbulence where you grew up."

Without turning around, Erica responds, "Iowa, I grew up in Iowa, George."

"Oh," responds George as he turns to continue his work.

But Eric Miller's heart pounds as he turns and looks at Dr. Myers who is not aware he is observing her and whispers to himself, "Erica Myers . . . Ricky!"

General Westbrook demands David Veil and Bill Rodgers accompany him to his office. Once there, General Westbrook slams the door and walks briskly to his chair and sits down. "I want an explanation and I want it now! *What the Sam Hill is going on here, gentlemen?* One minute the news is dreadful, the next minute you don't know. What the devil is going on here, and where is the *Argo Navis?*"

Bill Rogers drops his head, and David Veil throws his arms in the air and responds, "I honestly don't know, sir. Whatever our monitors had picked up simply vanished. Equipment malfunction is about the only logical explanation, sir. The *Argo Navis* on the other hand is moving at speeds that make it hard for us to track, especially using thirty-year-old technology. They have obviously deviated off their scheduled course, sir. We had them in a HALO about Venus before breaking orbit for Cygnus. We lost them just about the time the anomaly appeared."

"Find that ship now, gentlemen!" shouts General Westbrook. "I want to know the moment you reestablish communications with them."

David Veil and Bill Rodgers rapidly exit General Westbrook's office. Bill says to David as they walk back to the control room that he believes with all his heart this mission will end successfully and thinks General Westbrook believes this too. However, it must be embarrassing to call the president informing him the planet could be destroyed in just a few hours and then having to retract his statement. Bill replies that all he could think of an hour ago was that the *Argo Navis*, with its coed crew, was all that was left of humanity. Their fate was to keep humanity alive. Right now, the only thing that matter was finding that flying saucer.

A black limousine, bringing Elizabeth Devereaux to her father's Detroit home from the cemetery where he was buried, slowly pulls into her father's driveway. Elizabeth has opened Martin Devereaux's home for his neighbors who have provided food for those who have returned from the funeral service or stopped to pay their respect. Some of the women in the kitchen take Ms. Devereaux from room to room, introducing her to Martin's neighbors, former coworkers, and friends. Elizabeth realizes her father was well respected;

however, she feels like a guest in her father's home. Tired and exhausted, Elizabeth strolls into the living room to rest. Sitting in her father's recliner, she closes her eyes and puts up her feet. After a few moments, she overhears several women quietly converse about how they tried repeatedly, but unsuccessfully, to witness to Martin about salvation and being saved. Surprisingly enough, each woman has a different opinion of what is required for a person to enter into heaven. Minutes later, Elizabeth is fast asleep. The next thing Elizabeth knows, a woman awakens her.

"Ms. Devereaux, the ladies and I have put all the food away and cleaned your kitchen. We have left our telephone numbers on your refrigerator should you need or want to contact us. You should not wait too long before getting to bed. I'll lock the door behind me and check in on you tomorrow. We are so sorry for your loss. Martin was a good man, and one many of the widows around here will miss."

"Thank you so much for all you have done for me and for my father," extends Ms. Devereaux. "I truly could not have done this alone," explains a weary Elizabeth.

"Good night, dear," states the neighbor.

Elizabeth takes the neighbor's advice, retreats to her bedroom, undresses down to her underwear, and rolls into bed. Elizabeth asks God to assist her through this ordeal, to lead her and guide her in the direction he wants her to follow. Within seconds, she is sound asleep.

Elizabeth is sitting in a building she does not recognize but senses it is some kind of temple and belongs to God. She hears a man's voice beckoning her to come forward, but her eyes are focused on another man with outstretched arms. The man with his arms stretched out does not speak but instead is scanning the crowd, pausing briefly to look directly at her. She knows she has seen this man before but is unable to determine where. This scene continues to repeat itself until she slowly gets out of her seat and approach the man with outstretched arms. When she gets to him, she holds out her hands and places them in his. Then to her surprise, he calls her by name and wraps his arms around her. She closes her eyes and asks the man who she now believes to be an angel what he wanted her to do.

Elizabeth Devereaux leaps up in her bed, breathing very hard and attempting to catch her breath. She suddenly realizes she has just had a dream. For the first time in her life, she remembers her dream. "Oh, God," she cries, "what in the world is happening to me? I beg you, Lord, help me please!" With her hands covering her face, she begins to weep. "Oh, God, why have you taken my father away from me? Why have you taken the only family I had? What is happening to me? Why are you doing this to me? What have I done? Please tell me what I've done! For the first time in my life, I remember a dream and haven't a clue what it means. Oh, God, what did I do to deserve this? What do you want me to do? In my heart, I believe in you. I believe you are there. Oh, God, I beg you, show me the way. Please, God, help me!" prays Elizabeth repeatedly until she once again falls asleep.

The next few days, Elizabeth spends attending to her late father's affairs. She is impressed as to how well organized her father was and how prepared he was for death. He left for an inheritance everything he owned to his only daughter, Elizabeth. He left no bills for her to pay. He left a small chest with memories of him and his young daughter. As Elizabeth browses the many pictures and artifacts, she is overwhelmed with sorrow. She can only imagine how much her father loved her but cannot help but wonder why they did not stay in contact with each other more often. Elizabeth plans on liquidating all his assets but plans on treasuring the chest and its possessions forever. She rents a storage room out by Metropolitan Airport to temporarily store the items she will keep. She periodically recalls her dream and hopes one day its meaning will become clear.

In an Ann Arbor judge's chamber, Pat Richards's guilty plea to the hit and run vehicular homicide of Chuck Johnson is under review. Her attorney has been replaced by a government lawyer who is trying to get the charges dropped for her assistance in a larger conspiracy. The judge has allowed Pat Richards to visit with her husband in a room adjacent to his chambers.

"Pat, what the heck is going on here?" asks Raymond Richards, her husband of over thirty years. "After all these years, I don't really know you."

Pat Richards holds out her hand for her husband to take. Raymond reluctantly takes hold of it, and she pulls him toward her. "Sit, Raymond," she says. "To me all that matters is that you still love me as I love you. There are some things it is best you do not know. But one thing you can be assured of, and that is that deep down in my heart, I love you just as much today as the day we married. And I want to believe with all my heart that you love me too."

"Oh, Pat, you always know how to get to me," admits Raymond. "But you must know that all this comes as a shock to me. Husbands and wives do not keep such deep secrets from each other. I feel betrayed, Pat."

"One day, I hope you will find it in your heart to forgive me, dear," pleads Pat.

"Why can't that one day be today, honey?" asks Raymond.

"Because this is the way I want you to remember me, that I love you," begs Pat Richards with tears in her eyes.

"What do you mean remember you?" insists Raymond.

"Oh, Raymond, don't be so naïve. That man with the judge is not a lawyer for our government. He is also an international assassin. Should he have his way and take me into custody, I will not survive the night."

"Please, Pat, tell me what is happening. I can help you honey, if you let me."

"You are a good man, Raymond, and I love you; but let this go, I beg you!"

"I will not let it go, Pat. So you might as well tell me everything."

Pat Richards smiles at her husband, still grasping his hand. "Oh, what the heck, darling, seeing you will not let this go! Years ago, I studied music and the arts abroad, as a college exchange student. I was able to spend an entire year in Russia. My parents were so proud of their daughter, primarily because they did not have the money to send me to school, less known overseas. I know you know this, but what you don't know is that while in Russia, I got myself into a bit of trouble. Some girls and I got drunk one night and were responsible for the death of a prominent figure. A man I thought was an American diplomat working with the Russian Government assisted us and told me that he would keep in touch with me for one day I might return the favor, in duty to my country. As promised, he kept in touch with me and my whereabouts, and I performed minor assignments for him. It was through me that the Soviets knew about your work with Professor Mueller. This American diplomat I had come to trust was speaking Russian very fluently. I later learned he was actually a Russian citizen planted in the United States. The American diplomat/Russian spy you know as Walter Kennedy suspects his identity has been compromised and is going around covering his tracks. A few days ago, my latest assignment was to kill another Soviet operative, Chuck Johnson, and I now fear for my life because of what I know."

Raymond Richards is speechless as he stands and walks to a nearby window.

"Raymond, I'm so sorry. It's my fault the Soviets and Germans have detailed plans of your ship. I believe with all my heart they have built a vessel of their own. I believe they were going to use Chuck Johnson to sabotage your mission. I think someone possibly in the NIA is about to expose Director Walter Kennedy. With me out of the way, Walter Kennedy will likely disappear also, more than likely returning to Russia."

Turning his back to the window and facing his wife, Raymond asks, "Is that all?"

Briefly lowering her head, Pat looks directly at her husband and answers, "Yes, Raymond, I swear to you that is it, and that is the truth."

Raymond walks toward his wife and kneels at her feet. He grasps her hands in his and replies, "Pat, you could have come to me with this, you know."

"I was very afraid, Raymond. I was afraid of what these men would do to us if they found out I had discussed this with anyone."

"I understand, dear. But trust me, I can help you, and will help you."

"I believe in all my heart you will try, my husband, but don't get yourself killed over me," insists Pat Richards. "I must pay for what I've done."

Suddenly, a door opens and an agent enters the room. "Come with me, Mrs. Richards," he demands.

Raymond Richards follows his wife to the judge's chambers but could not enter. "Patricia Richards," states the judge, "I have been ordered to release you to the custody of the FBI. You are ordered to spend the night in the county jailhouse until expedition papers have reached my desk. Hopefully, this will take place no later than tomorrow afternoon."

The agent walks up to Pat Richards and whispers in her ear, "Did you say anything to your husband?"

"Yes," she replies. "I told him that I loved him."

The agent then motions for the officer to take her away.

Outside the judge's chamber, Raymond Richards watches as the police handcuff his wife and take her away, neither looking at the other. He then proceeds to the outside of the building and calls Professor Mueller, reaching him at his home. Professor Mueller asks him how everything went. Raymond Richards tells Professor Mueller everything his wife has told him. Professor Mueller asks Raymond to hold on as he contacts General Westbrook and conferences in him into the call with Raymond Richards. Professor Mueller instructs Raymond to repeat everything he has just told him to General Westbrook.

"Gentlemen, this confirms what I have already started to piece together," explains General Westbrook. "I have contacts in the NIA who have been following Walter Kennedy for months. Raymond Richards, for right now I want you to go home and act as if you know nothing, and by all means do not make any unusual phone calls from home. I'm not sure what, if anything, we can do to assist your wife, but we will take it from here." General Westbrook hangs up, and Raymond Richards says to Professor Mueller before disconnecting their communications, "Thank you, Hans. I do not have anyone else I can turn to." Professor Mueller replies, "No problem, Raymond."

The Truth Was from the Start

One of the engineers in mission control shouts, "I have them! I've found the *Argo Navis* . . ."

"Put it on the screen, man. Let's see it," instructs David Veil.

At first there are just blips on the huge screen millimeters apart.

"Man, she's really hauling butt. She's got to be doing seven or eight times the speed of light! Give me a second to reconfigure the screen's parameters so we can keep her in view. We've never tracked anything moving that fast before. Comparing their present course with what we were given from Dr. Myers, I should be able to display their current course vector in a smooth and steady trajectory. Check the viewing screen, not Mr. Veil."

From his communications console, another engineer announces his attempts to make contact with the spacecraft. *"Argo Navis*, this is Houston, do you read? Come in, *Argo Navis*." The communications engineer pauses for a moment and then repeats his message. *"Argo Navis*, this is mission control in Houston, please acknowledge! Dr. Myers, can you hear me?" The communications engineer automates his message so that it repeats every thirty seconds.

Dr. Erica Myers, Eric Miller, and George Lee sit at their respective consoles, unaware that the communications systems were disabled during their controversial discussions surrounding the course to Cygnus and possible early return to Earth. They are therefore unaware that the Space Agency is attempting to contact them.

Eric Miller having reviewed Dr. Myers navigational charts and courses does not sense a present danger and believes it is safe to turn off computer navigational control to see whether George can handle manually piloting the ship at hyperspeed. Dr. Myers asks George if he is ready, and he remarks, "As ready as I'm going to be, Doc. Make it so.

Just as George realizes the ship is on manual control, Erica Myers utters, "Oh my God! How long has this been off?"

A nervous George responds, "What's been off, Doc? Please don't tell me your auto navigation system has not been engaged, and no one has been piloting the ship!"

"I've just noticed the communications systems are offline. I'm not sure when they were turned off. I might have inadvertently shut them off when we were experiencing that turbulence problem," admits Dr. Myers as the systems come back online. There is silence on the bridge until suddenly a voice emerges from the speakers causing the crew to jump as if they were watching a scary movie. "*Argo Navis*, this is Houston, do you read?"

"Houston, this is the *Argo Navis*," acknowledges Dr. Myers. "We hear you loud and clear." Shrugging her shoulders with a smile on her face and putting the speakers on mute, she whispers to Eric and George, "I won't dare tell them the systems were offline."

Everyone in mission control shouts with joy and enthusiasm. David Veil then asks for silence as he instructs the communications engineer to open his microphone. "Dr. Myers, this is David Veil. We lost contact with you over a day ago and feared the worse. What's been going on out there?"

"Uh, Houston, this is Dr. Myers. On behalf of my crewmates, we'll have to get back to you on that one," inserts Erica once again shrugging her shoulders and muting the system.

In laughing disbelief, Eric Miller and George Lee both cover their mouths and stare at Dr. Myers. "We can't believe you just told your boss we'll have to get back to him, Doc. You are truly one of us now," proclaims George Lee shaking his head.

"Maybe I'll tell them we're just turning in for the night," suggests Erica.

Eric and George simultaneously look at their watches and nearly drown in tears holding back the laughter. "It's a little after 1:00 p.m. on Tuesday Erica," says Eric, desperately trying to maintain his composure while speaking. "Do you honestly think they'll buy it?"

By now, Dr. Myers has also been overtaken with joy. "Heck, guys, help me out."

Mr. Veil cannot believe the response he has just heard. He opens his mouth but no words proceed. After a minute, he requests, "Could you repeat that last statement, Dr. Myers?" He covers his headset microphone with his hand and asks for someone to call General Westbrook to the control room.

George suggests, "Okay listen, Doc. It's not really lying to say we're experiencing communications problems and in the process of correcting it." Turning to Eric, George elicits his opinion, "That's not really lying, is it bro?"

Before Eric can answer, Erica holds up one finger soliciting her crewmates silence and preparing to speak. "Houston, we have been experiencing communications difficulties but are confident the issues have been corrected. We are all fine, and the spacecraft and crew are performing very well. We are operating on manual control and will reestablish communications once we have plotted and confirmed a course back to Earth. *Argo Navis* out!" Erica immediately disables the communications system, again.

"Are you done, Doc?" asks George.

"I'm dead meat, guys," exhorts Erica.

"We had better start heading back, boys and girls," suggests Eric. "I do, however, have one more thing I would like to do, if it's all right with you two."

"And what might that be, Eric?" asks George continuing to pilot the ship. Not getting an immediate answer, George turns around and notices Erica is also waiting for a response from Eric.

"I would like you to navigate as close as possible into the asteroid belt, George. I would like to get a feel for what's there."

"Is this one of your experiments or has this some spiritual relevance?" asks a curious Dr. Myers.

"Actually, it's a little of both, my friends," replies Eric. A few moments pass by without anyone saying anything, anxiously waiting for Eric to expound. Sensing this, Eric reluctantly proceeds, "I realize this could be hard to believe, but I am hoping to sense and gather data relative to God's destructive wrath upon the fallen angels."

"Okay, Eric, I'm totally lost. Help me out here," requests Dr. Myers. "Do you believe God destroyed some angels in the midst of the asteroid belt?"

"Actually, I believe the asteroids between Mars and Jupiter were once a planet referred to in the Bible as Rahab. I believe the planet Rahab was a habitation for Lucifer and the angels. When they sinned against God, He totally destroyed their world."

"Man, that's pretty wild, Eric," states George. "I never knew God destroyed some of the angels. I would image you have scriptures supporting this?"

"Don't I always, G? Have you ever known me not to?" replies Eric. "But don't get me wrong, he only destroyed the planet. The angels that sided with Satan are bound awaiting they final punishment."

"I must say that's very interesting, Eric," interjects Dr. Myers. "This journey seems to be filled with your peculiar beliefs. I'm going to my quarters to get some rest. It's cool if you don't wake me when we get to the rocks."

"Did you say 'it's cool,' Doc?" asks George. "The longer you stay around us, the more you start to speak like us."

"Good night, you two," says Dr. Myers with a smile. "Don't stay up too late!"

Pat Richards sits quietly in a Washtenaw County jail cell. Out of the corner of her eye, she notices the female jailer walk past. She is surprised when the jailer starts to speak to her. "Get on your feet and away from the door, Mrs. Richards. You're free to go." As the keys jingle in the lock and the squeaky cell door opens wider and wider, Pat Richards's heartbeat races faster and faster as she validates her freedom.

"That's correct, ma'am. You're free," repeats the jailer. "You can pick up any belongings from the property clerk."

While gathering the few items she had at the time of her arrest, Pat Richards wonders how her freedom came about. She signs some papers and is escorted to the front of the police station. To her surprise, her husband is waiting and smiling. Raymond spreads his arms wide, welcoming his wife, who rushes to him and squeezes him tight.

"What do you say we grab a bite to eat, you must be starving," states Raymond. Reaching down on a chair beside him, he picks up a coat and drapes it around his wife.

"So when did you become a mind reader?" asks Pat Richards attempting to slip her arms into the sleeves of the coat. "Jesus, Raymond, what's this thing made of, lead?" The couple exits the police station arm in arm. Pat Richards turns to her husband, "I'm so sorry for all the pain and embarrassment I've caused you, Raymond. I never realized just how much you loved me until now. I should never have kept these secrets from you. But I tell you, I still fear for my life! Why do you suppose I am being set free?"

"It's all right, dear," Raymond reassures his wife. "Professor Mueller and General Westbrook are taking care of it."

"I guess it's time I started trusting you completely," admits Pat Richards drawing even more closely to her husband. "So where are you taking me for dinner?"

Raymond and Pat Richards walk to a popular downtown Ann Arbor restaurant to enjoy a meal and celebrate Mrs. Richards's unexpected release. The couple realizes it's been years since they have dined out and enjoyed a night away from home. They spend the next two hours enjoying their meal and each other's company. Having finished and paid for their meal, Raymond and Pat vacate the restaurant. Standing outside on the pavement in front of the restaurant, the two embrace each other like young lovers. Pat is curious when she notices a car approaching them very similar to Raymond's. "How thoughtful of you Raymond to have the valet bring the car around," she says.

An equally surprised Raymond Richards responds, "I didn't have anyone get the car, dear. This restaurant doesn't have valet parking."

Pat Richards's heart begins to pound and fear overshadows the memorable evening. Before either of them could take action, gunshots erupt from the passing vehicle, striking both patrons. Raymond and his wife fall to the pavement. The vehicle pulls to the curb and stops. Lying face down, Raymond stretches his bloody arm toward his wife. He notices a man approaching them from the car with what seems to be a handgun. He hears a very faint voice from the restaurant shout to call 911. The assailant retreats to the automobile and races away, as Raymond shuts his eyes. As the restaurant staff and customers exit the store to come to the couples aid, an ambulance races up. The restaurant manager makes a comment that the ambulance arrived before the police. An elderly male attendant and a young female paramedic quickly hoist the two victims onto stretchers and swiftly rush away. The restaurant manager is also at a loss of words as to why they rush off without turning on their lights or sirens. Seconds later, the police arrive and begin taking statements from witnesses. Moments later, an ambulance arrives and the paramedics demand to know where the victims were that required their attention. The police and restaurant manager are bewildered and stand mute.

Just around the corner at a pay phone, a man inserts some coins and dials a series of numbers. A gentleman on the other end answers the phone with hello. The caller in the phone booth starts his conversation, "Why did you hire a second assassin? Did you want to make sure it was done, or did you lose confidence in my abilities to do my job?"

In response, the voice on the other end insists, "Neither. I'm not sure what's going on. If you are confident your assignment was carried out, get back to Washington."

"Affirmative," says the caller from the phone booth then hangs up. Back in his office at the NIA, Walter Kennedy is convinced the Soviets have taken control of this situation by executing Pat and Raymond Richards before he had the chance to do so using his own operative. He is equally concerned that General Westbrook has exposed his cover and contemplates returning to the safety of Soviet soil.

Elizabeth Devereaux enters the office of a local apartment complex near Metropolitan Airport to sign a six-month lease. The landlord reads over her application and asks if Elizabeth Devereaux has a cellular phone in which she can be reached. After giving the landlord her number, she realizes that with a new battery in her cell phone, it works much better turned on. Once activated, she receives a flood of messages, many of which have come from her friend Helen Hayes. Elizabeth dials Helen's callback number and nervously waits as it rings. Within seconds, a soft voice answers, "Hello, this is Helen"

Very softly Elizabeth responds, "Hi, Helen. It's Elizabeth."

"Elizabeth, oh, baby, how are you? How is your father? I've missed you so badly, baby girl. Why haven't you called me?"

"Oh, Helen, I buried my father a few days ago, and I'm in the process of liquidating his entire assets. I've not had a battery charger for my cell phone, and my phone has been off, or else I would have phoned you. The only place I had your phone number was in my phone. Once I got my phone back on, I received your many messages. I'm sorry, Helen. But the truth is I knew you were there for me."

"So when are you coming home, baby?" inquires Helen.

"I'm not sure, Helen. I'm not sure when I'll be back."

Softly and sympathetically, Helen asks her friend; "Is there anything you'd like me to do for you, Elizabeth? Anything, anything at all?"

"No, Helen . . . I'm fine. Really . . . I'm fine. Thank you so much for asking and for caring about me." Starting to cry, Elizabeth continues, "I've got to go now, Helen. I'll call you in a few days."

Elizabeth Devereaux ends the call not knowing how to tell Helen the truth. Ever since her arrival in Michigan, something has been drawing her to stay, and she is determined to find it. She recalls the image of a man from her dream she had at her father's house and believes he will be able to assist her. She believes this man is in Michigan and will know him when she meets him.

"Approaching our solar system and slowing to sub-light speed. Asteroid belt in fifteen minutes," says George, as he turns in his chair to face Eric. "Are you serious about the rocks in the asteroid belt being the remnants of a destroyed planet?"

"Let me ask you something, George. Have you ever wondered what happened to the dinosaurs?"

George laughs replying "Not really, brother. They've been extinct for millions of years, and I'm cool with that. But maybe you didn't understand my question. What in the dickens does dinosaurs have to do with the asteroid belt being the remains of an ancient planet? You expect to find some bones there?"

Eric chuckles at George's comments then offers a more plausible explanation. "All I expect to find there is a sense of the truth."

"What truth?" asks George seriously.

"The truth about our planet Earth. As a Christian, I first believe God and the scriptures. As a scientist, I believe Earth leaves us clues to our existence. As a Christian scientist, I believe God is the one that has placed these clues for us, so that in the fullness of time, we might be able to explain truths hidden in the scriptures and hidden in the earth. God has allowed me to journey to this place in order to prove to me the truth about his wrath against the angels that aligned themselves with Satan and sinned against him. In his anger, God destroyed the planet Rahab, which we now see as the asteroid belt. Fragments or meteors from the explosion knocked the planet Earth of its axis and caused the extinction of the dinosaurs."

"And where do you find this in the Bible?" asks George.

Drawing closer to George, Eric answers, "In the first two verses of the Bible, between Genesis 1:1 and 2."

"That's amazing, Eric. I always love talking to you about the Bible," admits George. A proximity alert causes George to turn back to his command console. "We have arrived at the asteroid belt. I'll put us in an orbit parallel to the outer rim."

"Open the forward viewing portal, George," asks Eric as he concentrates on the portal. "Get us as close as you can to a rock, without endangering the ship."

George performs a slight pitch and roll maneuver, and suddenly gigantic rocks appear in the viewer catching them both by surprise and causing them to jump back.

"My God, my God," blurts out Eric.

"Are you sensing something, Eric?"

"I'm not really sure, George," replies Eric slowly stepping back from the portal. "I will be in my quarters praying, George."

"Don't forget to pray for me while you're at it," beseeches George.

On his way to his quarters, Eric replies without turning around, "I always do, my friend, I always do."

"How long do we stay here, Eric?" shouts George.

Just before closing the door to his cabin, Eric replies, "You'll know when, George."

George returns to gazing out the window at the phenomenal spectacle in space.

Minutes later, Dr. Myers emerges from her quarters, but George is unaware of her presence being hypnotized by the view. She slowly takes a seat at her navigational console and also witnesses the great rocks in space. "It's beautiful, isn't it, George? We're not too close, are we?"

"Oh yes, Doc. Ah, I mean, yes, it is beautiful, but no, we are not too close. We are in orbit roughly over five hundred miles outside the perimeter of the closest asteroid in the belt."

"You know we should be heading home soon?"

"Yeah, I know, Doc. We'll stay just a few more minutes. Eric told me I would know when the time to go would come."

"And you believe him?" asks Erica.

"Yes, I do, Doc, like you wouldn't believe. But you wanna know what's really strange? Ever since we discovered your leg was healed, I mysteriously started to believe in myself more than ever before. I have a confidence about myself that I can't explain." Then in a jovial tone, George proceeds, "I can't wait to get home and ask the first woman I see to marry me, or at least go out on a date. So yes, Doc, when Eric told me I would know when it's time to leave, I most definitely believe it."

"As a psychiatrist, George, I would question you more, but as a member of this crew, I too have experienced things I can't explain. This includes the miraculous healing of my leg and hip." An extremely solemn Erica Myers continues, "At first, I trusted Eric, but then his beliefs resulting in our debated retreat from Cygnus concerned me. Now I wish more than anything else I had the kind of religious insight he has."

"Christians call it faith," inserts George.

"I wish I had faith," admits Erica. "I wish I knew the Bible." After a brief pause, she continues, "Oh well, I should open a channel and reestablish contact with mission control."

"Yeah, Doc. You should. But you know that." George Lee returns to his console and slowly yet meticulously maneuvers the *Argo Navis* away from the asteroid belt with the assistance of Dr. Myers, who plots a course back to Earth.

Erica Myers successfully contacts the Space Agency, who has not lost the tracking lock on the spacecraft. The flight director voiced his concern when his staff noticed the *Argo Navis* was advancing dangerously close to the asteroid belt; however, Dr. Myers convinces them it was a planned maneuver. David Veil asks Erica to inform her crewmates that he, Bill Rodgers, and General Westbrook will meet them in Ann Arbor when they return for a postflight debriefing. George informs her that even at sub-light speeds, they will be in Earth's orbit within the hour. David Veil wishes her and her shipmates a safe landing. Dr. Myers acknowledges and assures her boss she will see him soon before severing their connection.

Erica Myers turns around sensing Eric Miller approaching from his quarters. "How long before we reach Earth?" asks Eric. Before George can acknowledge, Erica stands and walks toward Eric, grabbing him by the arm.

"I need to talk to you, Eric," she demands.

Shrugging his shoulders at George, Eric allows Erica to lead him to the lounge. Once there, Erica motions for Eric to take a seat while standing in front of him.

"How can I have faith, Eric?" asks Erica.

Swallowing and taking a deep breath, Eric responds, "Is this what you pulled me aside for?"

Pulling up a chair and sitting in front of him, Erica explains, "You have something that allows you to trust what you do not see. You have confidence to believe in something regardless of what others think. I'm not sure I'm saying this correctly, but I believe you have favor with God. I think he communicates with you and you trust what he tells you. George says Christians call it faith. How do *I* get faith?"

"The scriptures say faith cometh by hearing, and hearing the word of God. I think the first step is to read your Bible and ask God to open up your understanding to his word. Once you let God's word permeate your heart, you will begin to know what faith is."

"It seems like that could take a long time," suggests Erica. "Isn't there a three-to four-step process I could follow? I know nothing about the Bible, and I don't think I have the patience to read it."

"There is no step-by-step process. I sense something else is going on with you. It might not have anything to do with faith. It could be as simple as trusting your instincts."

"Trusting my instincts?" repeats Erica. "Trusting them how?"

"Your instincts told you to trust me in that continuing on our course to Cygnus would be devastating. I think your instincts are talking to you again. Most of the times in situations like this, I believe God is dealing with a person and using me as a guide."

"And where would you be guiding me?" asks Erica.

"Guiding you into his kingdom," says Eric.

"Am I not already in God's kingdom?" asks Erica.

"If you have to ask that question, it's a good chance you are not. But it's also a good chance God is opening up your heart to accept his plan of salvation."

"Right at this moment, I'm confused," admits Erica in a frustrated tone. "So let me ask you, Eric. How did you become a citizen of his kingdom?"

Eric explains, "The first thing was for God to open up my heart to his word and to believe in the works of his son, Jesus Christ, one must be born into this kingdom."

"I believe in Jesus," smiles Erica. "So what more is there?"

Taking hold of Erica's hand, "There is definitely something else going on with you, my friend," senses Eric. "Are you sure you are telling me everything?"

"Yes, Eric, at least pertaining to this subject, that is. To be honest, I am still having a hard time believing that by faith alone, you sensed danger in our continuing to Cygnus. I wish I had some kind of proof you were actually correct," admits Dr. Myers. "I wish I knew how to convincingly include this in my report. And most of all, I wish you knew me."

"Approaching Earth," shouts George looking back toward the lounge. "You need to strap in, boys and girls."

Erica gently pulls her hand away from Eric's and walks to her navigation station. Eric whispers softly, "I wonder why Erica would think I do not know her?"

General Westbrook has been in Ann Arbor all day. At present, his exact whereabouts are unknown as well as his companion, Professor Mueller. Yet everyone involved with this mission expects them on site at RNR Industries when the *Argo Navis* returns. The control tower at RNR Industries is made aware of the incoming flight of the *Argo Navis* from the Space Agency and has relayed telemetry data to them. Many of the employees of RNR Industries, EM Laboratories, and Mueller Engineering have gathered outside hangar 13, anxiously awaiting the safe return of their coworker astronauts. Using a secure channel, George contacts the control tower at RNR Industries and instructs them he will move the *Argo Navis* to a lunar orbit until night fall in the Great Lakes region. Afterward, he will make a rapid descent directly to the hangar attempting to avoid radar. The traffic controller confirms his actions and informs George Lee that the Space Agency and NORAD will assist in jamming area radar systems at that time.

Professor Mueller and General Westbrook pull up to the guard shack at RNR Industries in Professor Mueller's automobile. Once the guard waves them through, Professor Mueller parks in the lot in front of the main office building. They discuss the most pressing issue that concerns the coincidence between the Space Agency's loss of contact with *Argo Navis* and how that might relate to the belief in the destruction of the planet. However, their first priority is the safe return of the *Argo Navis* and its crew. David Veil and Bill Rodgers will be onsite in the next few hours. We'll use one of the conference rooms to debrief the crew. Professor Mueller acknowledges he will follow General Westbrook's lead. General Westbrook replies that he appreciates the kind gesture but thinks it best if Professor Mueller brought his team up to date on the state of affairs within his organization, mainly the situation with Pat and Raymond Richards and the future of RNR Industries. General Westbrook indicates he will concurrently read Dr. Myers's report before interviewing her. He would like for Professor Mueller be present at that interview, followed by separate interviews with George Lee and Eric Miller. Then they will get to the bottom of this conspiracy surrounding a second ship and the depth of Walter Kennedy's involvement with foreign governments. Professor Mueller nods his head in acceptance, and both men exit the automobile.

Walking into the building, General Westbrook and Professor Mueller are nearly knocked down by an enthusiastic employee rushing out of the building. In jubilation, he greets them and explains he is heading for the airport to pick up the flight director and his staff arriving from Houston. His haste results from an eagerness to return and greet his comrades.

Dr. Myers has retreated to her quarters finishing her logs and report. Eric Miller has been in the basement of the *Argo Navis* checking his engines. George has spent the past hour nervously pondering the reentry maneuver. He uses the ship's intercommunications systems to ask Eric if he wouldn't mind validating the warp to sudden-stop maneuver. While his confidence is high, he wants Eric to double check the engine firing sequences with his trajectory vectors.

Eric emerges from the basement to see Erica extending her hand to assist him. Eric takes her hand, and they look eye to eye at each other for a solid five seconds or so before Eric expresses his thanks for her assistance. Not knowing how to respond to Erica, Eric is relieved when George turns to them and remarks, "Hey,

you two. Eric, I really need your help understanding this warp to
sudden stop thing."

A confused Dr. Myers interjects, "Got all my paperwork done,
guys. What's going on?" as she straps herself into her seat. "What's
a warp to sudden stop?" She then looks to George who points to
Eric. "Well, Eric Miller, help me out," demands Erica.

"Well, Dr. Myers," giving an apathetic eye to George, "WTSS
or warp to sudden stop is a soon-to-be-tested theory that both
George and I designed and engineered. We know for example
that when a vehicle with occupants has a certain velocity abruptly
extinguished, the occupants within the vehicle retain their velocity
unless heavily restrained. If the restraining system is not sufficient,
the occupants will pass through the vehicle. If the restraining
system is sufficient but the force is not suppressed, the occupant
absorbs the force. Either way, the occupant does not survive the
sudden stop. The same thing happens to the vehicle. The system we
came up with basically uses the force for propelling the vehicle to
strengthen the vehicle's structure on sudden stop and exert an equal
but opposite force on the occupants. The force on the occupants
is diverted from the engines and routed into the ship's inertia-
dampening systems and chairs. The computers that control these
functions are untested. Likewise, the engines must work in concert
with the designated course; firing and braking systems have also not
been tested. Outside of being untested and extremely dangerous, I
don't have a clue why George is nervous."

"Well, George, you're not alone," admits Dr. Myers. "So why
again are we doing this?"

In a very comforting and reassuring manner, Eric continues, "For right now, we need to maintain secrecy. Therefore, we will initiate our warp engines for a millisecond pulse. The ship will hyperaccelerate from our orbit behind the moon and place us within miles over Ann Arbor, where we will hyperstop. This will cause us to return to Earth virtually unnoticed. We've had faith in each other so far, don't quit on me now."

"I'm sorry, Eric. I just have these horrible thoughts of all the old shuttle missions that tragically ended upon reentry," admits Erica.

Eric unbuckles his safety harness and goes over to George and gives him a big hug. "Enter in the coordinates for home, big guy." He then walks over to Dr. Myers and in like fashion embraces her. "All right now, Ricky . . ."

A surprised Erica turns her head and looks right into Eric nearly kissing him, puts both her hands on Eric's arms that are still around her, but cannot speak.

Eric kisses her on her forehead then continues, "Contact the Space Agency and the tower at RNR Industries and have them prepare for our arrival."

While strapping himself back into his seat, Eric and George prepare to perform their respective tasks.

Dr. Myers relays the information to the Space Agency and RNR Industries tower. She then looks back at Eric and waits for him to catch her eye. When he does, she softly acknowledges to him, "So this is what having faith is like!"

Eric winks at her, smiles, and nods his head, but in reality, he knows she is referencing natural faith, for spiritual faith has a totally different meaning. However, he does not want to ruin her joy. Eric Miller feels one day he might be able to use this natural experience of faith to explain spiritual faith.

George overhearing Erica's statement looks back at Eric and grins before letting out a big shout with his fist raised in the air, "Yeah, baby, let's do this!"

The car carrying David Veil, Bill Rodgers, and their driver pulls up and parks in front of the main office complex. "Come quickly," asks the driver opening the door to the building. Just inside, the driver holds out his arms signaling for them to stop as he hears the public address system activate.

"Attention all employees, attention please. *Argo Navis*, reentry in fifteen minutes. Please prepare yourselves accordingly. Emergency personnel, take your stations. This is not a drill. I repeat, this is not a drill."

The driver reverses his direction and instructs his guests to follow him. "Let's go back out the building and around past hangar 13. I'm really excited about this as you can probably tell."

Approaching the runway behind and adjacent to hangar 13, David Veil and Bill Rodgers notice General Westbrook and Professor Mueller in the midst of the crowd and walk over to them. General Westbrook acknowledges them by shaking their hands. He explains how they will review Dr. Myers's report while the crew decontaminates. He tells them Professor Mueller will need to talk to his crew about some issues that have developed with his organization, after which they will all sit down and determine where they go from here. He also ensures them that this process will not be completed tonight. Someone in the crowd cries out, "Any minute now," as all eyes are focused on the clear, dark, star-studded sky. You can cut the crowd's anxiety with a knife. Heads and eyes move slightly surveying the heavens, not knowing exactly where the spacecraft will appear. Eric's friend, Grace, points to a spot in the sky, "This is where they will appear," she predicts.

"And how can you be sure of that?" asks someone standing next to her.

Grace replies without taking her eyes off the sky, "I hear they are coming from the moon. There's the moon, and if I know George, he will take the most direct path."

Suddenly, a flash of light rips open the dark sky, long enough to reveal a black saucer-shaped object before fading away.

Mixed emotions and feelings emerge from the crowd. "That was the *Argo!*" someone says. "Yeah, I think I saw it too," replies another.

"I don't think so," say others. "If it were the *Argo*, where is she?"

"The ship is black, the sky is black, just give it another second," whispers Grace.

A sonic boom is heard coming from the end of the main runway. Everyone bends down as hearts beat faster and faster. "What the heck was that?" they collectively murmur.

"Look, there she is. The *Argo Navis* is over near the tower," shouts Grace. The ship slowly and quietly maneuvers toward hangar 13. Professor Mueller cries out, "Clear a path and open the hangar doors. Make sure everyone is out of the hangar and set decontamination countdown to thirty minutes."

"You can open your eyes now, Dr. Myers," insists Eric Miller. George has opened the forward viewing portal. "Take a look, we're back on Earth. We're home."

"I might not have always shown it, but from the very first time I met your acquaintance in the lobby at the Space Agency, I knew you two guys were my friends, and I trusted you. We have something special, and I really don't want this journey to end," admits a teary-eyed Dr. Myers.

"Who says this is going to be the end?" questions George. "I believe this is just the beginning, not the end."

"I agree, George," states Eric. "Our journeys here and there have just begun. Truly, God has blessed us and will continue to do so. How soon till we dock, G?"

Swiveling around to access his control panel, George responds, "Twenty meters from hangar 13. *Argo Navis* ready to accept hangar umbilical system. We should start decontamination shortly, which should last another twenty-five minutes."

"Will we have to stay on the ship during decontamination?" asks Dr. Myers.

"Yes," answers George. "We'll remain on the ship for a few hours. However, we will be able to communicate with the control tower where equipment has been installed to monitor our condition as well as that of the ship. As you might know, we are also concerned about having brought back any foreign and/or hostile elements."

"Well, George, I feel better now," sarcastically admits Dr. Myers with a hint of humor. "Will it be possible to send my bosses my report?"

"Sure enough, Doc. You can upload your report to the tower's computers along with Eric's experiments and flight data from the ship."

Erica turns up the volume on her earpiece. "I'm getting something over the communications systems. Going to ship-wide audio."

". . . back home, *Argo Navis*. Please acknowledge that you are all safe and cognizant."

"Glad to be back, tower," replies Dr. Myers.

The tower traffic controller replies, "Decontamination procedures starts in T minus sixty seconds . . . get some rest . . . please finish and make your reports and logs available within the hour . . . e-briefing at zero six hundred hours . . . again, welcome home."

MYSTERIES AND DESTINIES UNFOLD

E very employee of Mueller Engineering, EM Laboratories, and RNR Industries are assembled outside hangar 13, waiting to enter and congratulate the crew of the *Argo Navis*. With a rock concert-type mentality, they shout and yell the names of Eric Miller, George Lee, and even Dr. Erica Myers. Any minute now, the decontamination process will end, and they are expecting to be cleared to go into the hangar. They have been promised the opportunity to reunite with their colleagues once the quarantine has been lifted.

Inside the *Argo Navis*, Eric, George, and Dr. Myers patiently wait for their release, knowing it will be their fellow associates who will signal the end to their lockdown.

"What's the first thing you guys will do when we are cleared?" asks Erica.

George is quick to respond. "That's easy, Doc," he says as he heads toward the exit hatch, "I'm heading straight for the cafeteria and the coffee pot!"

Eric laughs and walks over to meet George at the hatch. "The first thing I plan on doing is thanking God for blessing us to set foot back on Earth. Other than that, I think I'll join George for a couple or three cups of grog. So what are you going to do, Erica?"

"Well, I'm not really sure. I guess that's why I asked you two. I'll probably follow you two into the cafeteria. To tell you the truth, I feel like a stranger here. I believe your comrades are wonderful people, but I'm not sure they will welcome me as they do you."

"I understand why you might feel that way, Erica; however, give these folks a chance," pleads Eric. "I think you'll be surprised. Remember, you are part of our family now, and they know that. George and I know these people, Erica. Don't worry, they will embrace you. Just flow with it. You'll be fine."

George is excited as he motions with his hands for his comrades to see. "Look, guys, a crowd is gathering around the ship. I think it's time us sardines jump the can."

With Eric Miller sandwiched between Dr. Erica Myers and George Lee, they wrap their arms around one another like childhood chums. They can hear the crowd counting down from ten. Once they reach zero, they repeatedly shout in unison, "Come on out, come on out, come on out, come on out . . ."

All eyes in hangar 13 are on the *Argo Navis*, in particular the area they believe to be the exit hatch, aware they will not see the hatch actually open. What seems like eternity ends when George Lee magically emerges from the side of the black spacecraft and gives a wave to the crowd. A huge cheer and applause immediately erupts. Right behind him is Eric Miller. He too receives an enormous reception. Eric then extends his arm into the HALO hatch and seizes the hand of his female crewmate. When Dr. Erica Myers appears, the crowd goes wild with whistles and expressions of gratitude that nearly brings tears to Dr. Myers eyes. George and Eric also clap their hands on Erica's behalf, and then all three Argonauts wave their hands while walking down the ramp. At the bottom of the ramp, Eric Miller stops and motions for the crowd to quiet down. When they do, he drops to his knees and silently starts to pray. Everyone in the crowd quietly and without reservation closes their eyes and bows their heads. Those who know how to pray, pray. Others simply bow their heads out of respect. After a few moments of silence, Eric rises from his knees, thanks God through Jesus's name, and says "Amen." The first person to greet him is his friend Grace. She hugs him, then George, and with a sustained hug, Dr. Myers, making Erica feel very welcomed. Grace then hooks her arm through Erica's and pointed toward the main complex where General Westbrook and Professor Mueller were waiting to personally congratulate each of them.

As the crowd walk to the main building, George asks if he could please stop and get a cup of coffee. Grace informs him that an entire meal has been prepared in their honor. She told them there are tables set up just for them in front of the podium. They are all heroes, and the staff of RNR Industries are prepared to serve and honor them.

The crowd that inundated them with congratulations now prepare to serve the astronauts as they take their seats at the honorees table. Within seconds, George and Eric are both handed a long awaited cup of hot coffee. During the next half hour, all present at the celebration eat and attempt to give the astronauts some breathing room. Professor Mueller, General Westbrook, David Veil, and Bill Rodgers all get a chance to speak to the Argonauts as they finish their meal and start to mingle. Erica is extremely proud to have her new colleagues from the Space agency in attendance and supporting her. The informal celebration continues for about thirty minutes until Professor Mueller steps to the microphone and requests the crowd's attention. He also requests that Eric Miller, George Lee, and Dr. Myers come forward and return to the guest table. Professor Mueller also invites the delegation from the space administration to a table prepared especially for them. Before taking his seat, Professor Mueller announces that the successful maiden voyage of the *Argo Navis* will pave the way for a new parent company formed from the collaboration between RNR Industries, EM Laboratories, and Mueller Engineering. George Lee and Eric Miller are surprised and look around for Raymond Richards. General Westbrook takes the podium next and promises the audience that the space administration would contract with the new company to manufacture a fleet of hyperspeed spacecraft. General Westbrook finally gives thanks for everyone's support and asks Eric Miller, George Lee, and Dr. Erica Myers to prepare themselves for a postmission briefing.

Elizabeth Devereaux's cellular phone rings and when she answers finds her friend Helen Hayes on the other end. Helen asks how Elizabeth is doing and if she has a minute. After Elizabeth responds that she is doing fine and for Helen she has two minutes, Helen could not wait to tell Elizabeth is happening right there in Michigan.

Helen starts by informing Elizabeth that the guys from Michigan were some kind of astronauts and engineers, built a spaceship capable of light speeds, and flew it on some mission with the assistance of General Westbrook, the flight director, and his staff, and they just so happen to be in Ann Arbor right now. She asks Elizabeth if she knows where Ann Arbor is, not realizing that the hospital where her father died is in this city.

Elizabeth interrupts her friend, "Calm down girl, where are you at and how did you come about this information?"

"I'm at home right now, Elizabeth," says Helen. "Most essential personal were given a briefing on Friday once the mission was nearing its final stages. We were also told this information is still highly confidential. Can you believe this? These guys were just here among us and what about that new doctor?" Helen pauses for a second awaiting a response from Elizabeth. When there is silence on the other end, Helen repeats, "Hey Lizzy, you there? Are you all right?"

"Uh, yeah, Helen, I'm here and I'm okay. Something you said just triggered something in my mind. Got to go, but I'll get back to you." Elizabeth folds up her cell phone and searches her apartment for her purse. The word hallelujah keeps coming to her mind. Her lips and tongue start to quiver, and a mysterious warmth blankets Elizabeth. Her body starts to tingle and pulsate as unrecognizable words come uncontrollably out of her mouth. This sensation comes and goes for the next few minutes. She abandons the search for her purse and instinctively activates the voice recorder on her phone just seconds before the unexplained speech returns.

Leaving the celebration, the crew of the *Argo Navis*, Professor Mueller, General Westbrook, Mr. Veil, and Mr. Rogers proceed to the main conference room. This particular conference room is the largest of several within this facility, and the most technologically equipped. Adjacent to the main conference room is a smaller room where guests wait prior to entering the main room. A hidden camera in the guest room is connected to a monitor in the main room, along with a two-way intercom system. A fully stocked beverage bar sits in a remote corner of the main conference room. Perched in the middle of the room is a large oval conference table, large enough to seat over twenty people. General Westbrook, Professor Mueller, David Veil, and Bill Rodgers sit on one side of the table, while Eric Miller, Dr. Erica Myers, and George Lee take seats opposite them, with Dr. Myers in the middle.

General Westbrook starts the interviews. "There are a few things Professor Mueller and I thought he should share with just George Lee and Eric Mueller, but seeing you three have formed a tight bond, we will inform you as a team. I also see no need to exclude David Veil and Bill Rodgers from this knowledge. Afterward, we will need to interview each of you separately before bringing you back as a team for a final briefing. Let me first of all congratulate you three on a very successful mission. We will coordinate a systematic release of information over the next few months to the media for the general public. As Professor Mueller stated earlier, we will negotiate a contract between our government and a new incorporated company Professor Mueller will address in a few moments."

"Thank you, General Westbrook," says Professor Mueller. "As General Westbrook has indicated, we want to update you all as a team. No doubt George, you and Eric might have noticed the absence of Raymond Richards. You may or may not be aware of the fact that the Chuck Johnson, who was employed at RNR Industries, was an imposter implanted in our organization to steal classified information relative to the hypership project. This man was allegedly slain by Raymond Richards's wife, Pat. It appears as if Pat had ties with the Russians through a double agent within the NIA, who held her life in ransom for her assistance. The double agent is believed to be the NIA director Walter Kennedy. General Westbrook will go into more details concerning the NIA director. Ann Arbor police charged Pat with the murder of Chuck Johnson but afterward released her. Officially speaking and very much off record, Pat and Raymond Richards were gunned down outside an Ann Arbor restaurant."

George and Eric lean forward and look at each other in disbelief. "Pardon me, Professor," interrupts a visibly shaken Eric Miller; "Raymond and his wife are dead?"

"Officially speaking, Mr. Miller," replies Professor Mueller.

"Why do you keep saying 'officially speaking,' Professor?" asks George.

"Officially, we suspect NIA director Walter Kennedy sent an assassin to silence Pat Richards," continues Professor Mueller. "General Westbrook and I intervened and sent our own agent to carry out the assignment officially."

"So let me get this straight, Professor," says Eric. "Officially they are dead. And why would we sanction a hit on the Richards?"

Scratching his head, Professor Mueller admits, "I carried out the execution."

"You killed them, Professor?" asks George solemnly.

"I shot them, George, but they are not dead. They had on bulletproof clothing. I had to wound them to make it appear the sanction on their lives had been carried out. That is the unofficial story that must not leave this room. Our colleagues will be informed at a later date. George will fly them out of this facility when he takes Dr. Myers back to her mother's home. Right now, they are recovering from their injuries on board the Lear jet. The same aircraft you will use to escort Dr. Myers to Iowa. We have an apartment across the Mississippi River in Rock Island. They will stay there indefinitely."

Dr. Myers then asks why George would be flying her back to Iowa.

General Westbrook pauses and takes a deep breath. "The incident with Pat and Raymond Richards was not the only tragedy that took place while you were gone. I've never been good at delivering bad news with compassion, so please forgive me for being blunt, but I deeply regret to inform you, Dr. Myers, of the passing away of your mother. I had intended to inform you of this privately, but the opportunity never presented itself."

Erica shakes her head in disbelief and raises her hands to her face, trying desperately to hold back tears. Both Eric and George put their arms around her and embrace their partner. Seconds later, in the tradition of a seasoned soldier, she raises her head, takes a deep breath, and signals for General Westbrook to resume.

"The preliminary cause of death appears to be from a heart attack. After we convene here as Professor Mueller has indicated, he will have Mr. Lee fly you to Iowa while Mr. Lee attends to the

Richards. Again, Doctor, please accept our deepest condolences." General Westbrook then points to Professor Mueller to continue.

"Finally, concerning RNR Industries," explains Professor Mueller, "Raymond Richards has signed over all legal ownership documents to me. We will form a new company incorporating EM Laboratories, should Eric Miller consent, along with Mueller Engineering into the new RNR Industries LLC." Professor Mueller suggests this is a good point to take a break and let George Lee, Eric Miller, and Dr. Erica Myers digest everything they have just heard. He asks the three of them to exit to an adjacent guest conference room before they start the individual interviews.

George, Eric, and Erica, still startled from the tragic news of their friends and family, head into the guest room. Once inside, Erica breaks down and cries. George, wanting to do something but not sure how to react, just drops his head and asks repeatedly how all of this could be happening when things seem to be going along so well. Standing close to Erica, Eric, having lost both his parents, passionately embraces her.

Professor Mueller activates the closed-circuit monitor, lowers the sound in the conference room, and asks his colleagues to observe.

Eric Miller, while embracing Erica, whispers in her ear, encouraging her to cry, and praying secretly to God to bless her. Eric then releases his embrace, guides her to a chair, takes a seat beside her, and holds her hand.

Allowing Eric to still hold her hand and staring at the floor, Erica Myers admits, "Right now, I can't seem to think straight or do anything. I'm afraid I won't be too impressionable in an interview."

"I've got a feeling you'd be majestic in any situation, Ricky," encourages Eric, deliberately using her childhood nickname.

George, standing in a corner pondering all that has transpired surrounding this mission, turns toward Eric and Erica after hearing Eric refer to Dr. Myers as Ricky. A surprised Dr. Myers also looks up at Eric, her heart rate starting to increase. "You called me Ricky, Eric. Ricky was my nickname as a child. My father gave me that name, but only my mother still calls or called me by my nickname. The only way you could have known that was to have known me as a child. So I ask you, Eric, how could you have possibly known that?"

"I think you know the answer to that, Erica. As a matter of fact, I think you've known who I was well before I figured out who you were," admits Eric.

George walks over to where Eric and Erica are sitting, pulls up a chair, and takes a seat. "What in the name of God are the two of you talking about?" he asks.

"Now just how interesting is this becoming?" asks Professor Mueller. "Let's see where this is going. Now we're getting a glimpse into why they support each other like they do. This will be interesting, gentlemen."

General Westbrook concurs, "That's why you became a professor and I'm just a dumb old general. I too am interested in seeing how this little mystery unfolds."

Eric looks at Erica, who nods for him to proceed. "Well, George, it's like this," starts Eric, constantly focusing his eyes on Erica. "Back in the midsixties, the company my father worked for transferred my family from southeastern Michigan to a little city in western Illinois. My father's first challenge was to find a home for us. Due to racial segregation, we were forced to live in Iowa. Even there, the challenges continued for my family. I was forced to attend a school miles away from my home, where other nonwhite minorities attended. While it is easier to cope with societies' problems, I still battled blatant prejudges. I could not hide the color of my skin. Nevertheless, my father wanted my siblings and me to participate in events without fear. It was at one such events, a roller skating party, I discovered someone with whom I could relate to. Someone who like myself was also noticeably different. Not to brag, but I skated better than any of those kids, but I did not have a partner. I skated forward and backward, sometimes dancing to the music, but always with my eyes on this really pretty girl sitting all alone with her roller skates on but not getting on the floor. I would skate past her and wonder why she would not get up and skate with the rest of the kids. Then it hit me. She was the girl in class that wore the braces on her legs and walked with two canes. Upon further examination, I could see her braces on her legs. No one was ever going to ask her to skate because she could not skate. In a similar fashion, no one was ever going to skate with me. I felt so bad for her but realized she was content just to be at the party. This of course was not enough for me. I thought to myself, if you are such the expert skater, you could assist her."

As Eric continues, tears start to roll down Erica's face. For the first time, she gets an account of that event from Eric's perspective.

"So I rolled past her, circled back, and stopped right in front of her," continues Eric. "She looked right up at me and smiled. I believed I frightened her when I held out my hand for her to join me. She dropped her head then looked me straight in my eyes and very politely said, 'I can't skate.' I nervously asked her if she trusted me. She very girlishly replied, 'I don't know, I guess.' So I helped her up, got her balanced, and told her to just hold on to me and trust me, and we were going to have some fun. So I stood her up and told her to get on my right side. I felt if something happened, she would be on the outside of the rink floor. I could feel her nervous body shiver. To keep her up, I placed my right arm around her waist, and she held on to it with her right arm, with her left arm secured tight around my waist. We then started onto the floor moving ever so slowly. By now, we had captured everyone's attention. Mostly everyone moved out of the way for us, but a few knuckleheads raced past us, brushing me slightly. I could hear some kids start to murmur and tease us, but I just blocked them out. The more I heard them, the more pumped up I became. The more they stared at us, hoping the crippled girl would fall, the more determine I became. After our first complete round, all eyes were on us. I could feel her start to relax. Before we could complete another trip around the rink, the rink announcer put on a slow love song. I then popped the question and asked her what her name was. She said, 'My name is Erica, but my dad calls me Ricky.' I asked her if I could call her Ricky, and she said yes. To my surprise, someone started clapping, and then everyone joined in. The other kids started to pair up and skate behind us, and no one passed us. As the song got near its end, I took both her hands into mine, held them tightly, and faced her skating backward. The song ended, and we stopped. Ricky said her legs were starting to get tired. I sat down next to her, and to my amazement, all the kids stopped by to congratulate us. It was the first time I felt a part of the community. It was also the first time I felt love."

"Wow, man, that was beautiful," replies George. "What happened next?"

"Well, what happened next was not so beautiful," admits Eric. "Ricky said, 'Thank you, Eric.' I asked her how she knew my name, and her response was that everybody knew the little 'colored' boy. My day had given me a dollar, and it was burning a hole in my pocket. I asked Ricky if she wanted a soda, and she said yes. I skated to the vending area to get a couple pops out of the machine, and a man approached me. He told me that the girl I was skating with was his daughter. I started to get a little nervous when he went into his pocket. He came out with change, put it into the machine, and told me to make a selection and then to make the next selection for his daughter. He told me to take it to her. Right about then, I felt fairly relieved. That is until he put his hand on my shoulder and said, 'You enjoy the rest of the evening, boy, but I do not want you to ever skate, dance, or even as much as talk to my daughter after this day.' And out of fear, his wishes did I honor. I enjoyed the beverage with Ricky, my dad picked me up an hour or so afterward, and within a month or so, we moved back to Michigan. For a year or so, I thought about Ricky, wondering if I would ever see her again, wondering if I could ever feel that way about someone again. But over time, she faded away. Now fate has reunited us."

"So when did you figure out that Dr. Myers was Ricky?" asks George.

"Not until we were heading back to Earth, George. You asked Erica to finish telling us where she was from. Dr. Myers said she was from Iowa. She also mentioned something to the effect that she wished I knew who she was. It was then," admits Eric, "I knew Dr. Erica Myers was Ricky."

"I knew you two had something going on, man. I could see how you two interacted with each other," explains George. "And what about you, Doc, how long have you known Eric was the little (what was it they called you guys back then, crayons or something), sorry, man," teases George with a little laugh.

Still holding Eric's hand and looking him straight in the eye, Dr. Myers admits, "I knew it from the first time I interviewed Eric in my office in Houston and he told me he once lived in Iowa. I was so certain and nervous that I had to excuse myself to the restroom."

"So that explains why you left your office," remembers Eric. "At that time I had no idea who you were. Yet I must admit Ricky, I have sensed something about you, even when we encountered each other at the convenience gas station in Texas the morning of our interview."

Dr. Erica Myers takes her hands, places them on Eric Miller face, and responds, "I am so sorry for my father's actions. I often wondered why you refused to talk to me in school the following weeks after the skating party. Our teacher told the class you moved away, so I figured I would never see you again. To this day, no one has ever shown me that kind of compassion. Ever since that day, you set a standard for men that was never matched."

"This is unbelievable," admits Professor Mueller, "but I think it's time we invite the *Argo Navis* crew back into the room." Just as Professor Mueller prepares to use the two-way intercom system to summon George, Eric, and Dr. Myers back into the main conference room, General Westbrook's cell phone rings. Professor Mueller, David Veil, and Bill Rodgers remain quiet as to not disturb General Westbrook while he answers his phone. After roughly a minute of nodding his head, positively acknowledging the caller, General Westbrook ends his call, folds his phone, and returns it to his coat pocket without as much as whispering a word.

"Thank you, Professor, for waiting, but please bring our guest back into the conference room." Without hesitation, Professor Mueller depresses a button on the intercom and asks the *Argo Navis* crew to rejoin them. Once in the room, they resume their previous seating arrangements. General Westbrook gives a nod to Bill Rogers, signaling his approval to proceed.

"Well, gang, thanks for being patient and giving us time to compare our notes. I think the best place to start is at the beginning," states Bill Rodgers as he thumbs through their reports. "It seems as if this mission might have had some problems even prior to liftoff. Eric Miller, your report differs from George Lee and Dr. Myers in that yours is the only one that mentions an incident with locking caps on the fuel injectors. Please explain."

"Sure, Mr. Rogers, I can't explain why my crewmates failed to record this incident outside of trying to protect me. However, I assure you they meant no harm, and I explained it to them as well. Nevertheless, it was a very big deal and could have led to the destruction of the vessel."

General Westbrook moves very close to the table and folds his hands in front of him as to not miss a single word that Eric might say. His change in disposition is noticed and felt by everyone in the room, yet he remains silent.

Eric Miller explained that he left this project after suspecting his work might have been compromised due to a break-in as his laboratory. Highly specialized and engineered fuel injectors in his lab were stolen and replaced with cheap replicas, and the original engine design blueprints were replaced by copies to match the poorly designed injectors. I did not share this information with local police. The original fuel injectors that my lab designed and manufactured had manually controlled locking caps, but the original blueprints indicated that the caps would be automatically disengaged when the engines were brought online under computer control. I had planned to give George the schematics for incorporating the electronic locking cap release technology into the computer systems prior to my leaving the program but simply forgot. While the faulty fuel injectors had nothing to do with the locking caps, it reminded me that the caps had to be manually disabled in order for the antimatter stream to flow from the containment cells through the injectors. Otherwise, the ship would blow."

"So why did you not inform Mr. Lee of this after you returned to the program?" asks David Veil.

"I guess I just forgot," replies Eric.

"Do you believe these locking caps are necessary in future fuel injector designs?" asks Bill Rodgers.

"Absolutely," replies Eric. "Absolutely."

General Westbrook breaks his silence and astute attention and asks Eric, "This is well and good, Eric Miller, and it seems as if you saved your life and the life of your crewmates. But isn't it true you knew all along about this problem and kept silent knowing that if anyone attempted to use your technology, they would be destroyed?"

"Absolutely not, General," replies Eric in a calm demeanor.

"Then I want to thank you, Eric Miller, for opening up my understanding. An operative of mine in the NIA assigned to track the whereabouts of Director Walter Kennedy lost him somewhere in western Germany. Moments ago, I received a call that there was a high-energy explosion in the region where we suspected the Germans were building the second ship. The energy signature matched that produced by your antimatter engines. It's also just a few kilometers from Walter Kennedy's last known location. While the German and Russian governments are attempting to fabricate a cover story, I believe it's safe to say that your locking cap secret has guaranteed the *Argo Navis* its uniqueness."

"How can you be so sure it was the second ship?" asks Eric.

"Believe me, Mr. Miller; the energy signature produced by your engines is unique. We are verifying this as we speak."

"And you believe Walter Kennedy was in the area?" asks Professor Mueller.

"I'll go even further to say he was on board," states General Westbrook. "Many in the scientific community believe warp travel has medical benefits. I would have called Walter Kennedy a fool for believing this if I had not know Dr. Myers left here with a limp and has returned without one. Dr. Myers, do you mind shedding some light on this?"

Dr. Myers simply told them that Eric Miller prayed for her let to be healed and she believes that is exactly what happened, and it had nothing to do with warp travel.

General Westbrook continues by telling Dr. Myers he will accept her explanation for now but asks her to explain what happened approximately sixty hours into the flight.

A bewildered Dr. Myers has no idea what General Westbrook is referring to, so he asks David Veil to share with the three astronauts what mission control experienced roughly sixty hours into the flight.

All eyes turn to David Veil as he informs the crew of the *Argo Navis* that they lost contact with your ship approximately two and a half days into the mission.

"I admit, sir, we might have had some communications issues, but I assure you we did not . . ."

Mission Control and Flight Director David Veil abruptly interrupt Dr. Myers. "Please, let me finish, Doctor. We at Mission Control didn't just lose communications with your ship. Bill Rodgers, will you activate the projection screen as I upload the video log of the control room from my notebook? To save time, I'll move these frames along at ten times the normal speed." Using a laser pointer, David Veil points to the tracking screen. "This line represents the trajectory of *Argo Navis* fifty hours after liftoff. Just after you left the solar system and before we could recalculate your position, this started," pointing to the far right side of the trajectory map.

The three *Argo Navis* astronauts stare intensely at the screen, attempting to focus on what David Veil is pointing at.

"So you temporarily lost our position," states Dr. Myers, noticing the absence of the light blip indicating the *Argo Navis* spaceship. "Is that your cause for alarm?"

"Just give it some time, people," suggests David Veil. "You'll see."

"All I see is darkness," inserts George Lee, pointing to the right side of the screen. "Was there some kind of malfunction with the equipment? It's as if the stars are starting to disappear."

"That's a very interesting observation, Mr. Lee. Is there anything else you notice? Oh, and no, the equipment was not malfunctioning."

"The darkness seems to be growing," adds George Lee.

"Exactly!" shouts David Veil. "Phone calls came in from every deep space observatory on the planet. The phenomenon was starting to grow exponentially, and we calculated at that time it would have swallowed our solar system and Earth in less than nine hours. Our only thoughts were that *fate* had placed you three together to repopulate the human race, whatever world you might have discovered to call home."

Eric Miller, George Lee, and Dr. Erica Myers look on in disbelief. "So what did you do?" asks Dr. Myers. "How were you able to overcome or defeat this thing?"

"We did nothing," answers David Veil as he advances the tape to seventy-two hours after liftoff. "Now look closely. Literally minutes before our demise, there you see, it just vanished. Also notice that the mission clock is right at seventy-two hours after liftoff."

"So why are you showing this to us?" asks George Lee.

General Westbrook interjects, "As we studied your reports and the ship's logs, we were blown away by the fact that Dr. Myers made entries into her log that correspond to the exact times the phenomenon appeared and then just as mysteriously disappears. So once again, Dr. Myers, I ask you, what was going on between sixty and seventy-two hours into the flight?"

George Lee and Dr. Erica Myers look at Eric, who with his head lowered has started quietly praying and thanking God.

"This is unbelievable," whispers Dr. Myers.

"What's that, Dr. Myers? Could you speak up so we can hear you?"

Dr. Myers once again looks at Eric. Sensing this, Eric opens his eyes, looks back at Dr. Myers, and whispers for her to go ahead and tell them.

"Well, sir, I left certain facts out of my logs and report because of conversations I was having with Eric Miller. I did not want to make waves over something I thought was irrelevant. We were having a disagreement of sorts, between his beliefs and mine. But now in retrospect, I must admit, maybe he was right."

"Right about what, Doctor? Please get to the point!" insists General Westbrook.

"After leaving Venus's orbit, we decided to head to Cygnus," explains Dr. Myers, looking at Eric. "To make a long story short, Eric was opposed to this course stating that, well, that he believed he was chosen to this mission to prevent the destruction of another world. The way he explained it, all space is like a garment, and this region of space was like a zipper on the garment. Since the creation of eternity, the zipper has been closed. Our ship, however, acted like the lever of the zipper and started opening space. In the same fashion as a zipper folds open from the lever, so it was that our space was folding open behind us as we moved forward. As the lever of the zipper is the only common factor to both sides of the garment, so was the *Argo Navis* the only common factor to both sides of space. Everything that we knew was being turned inside out." Turning her head and now looking at General Westbrook, Dr. Myers continues, "And that small world we were destroying was Earth. We reversed our course approximately ten hours later, in effect closing the zipper and returning this delicate part of time space to normal."

Eric reaches for and grasps Erica's hand and smiles, giving his approval for her rendition of the event.

"That's amazing, Dr. Myers," insists David Veil. "Do you actually believe this?"

"As a doctor on this mission to observe the crew's behavior, I did not believe Eric Miller to be suffering from some kind of mental breakdown or to be delusional," adds Dr. Myers. "Eric's sincere belief was enough to convince me to change our course. As crazy as it appeared at the time, I'm glad I listened to him. I would hate to think what might have happened if we had not." Once again turning and looking at Eric, Erica continues, "One thing I know for sure is that I would travel into space with this crew anytime because we believe and trust one another."

"So how do we categorize this incident?" asks Professor Mueller. "As successful as this mission seems to have been, in order for the program to continue, we must return to space."

George Lee and Dr. Erica Myers look at Eric Miller to answer the question.

"I thank God for giving me the vision to avert this tragedy and the respect of my shipmates. I agree we must move forward with space exploration but suggest this delicate region of space be quarantined and designated off-limits," replies Eric.

"Is this possible to control?" asks David Veil.

"Right now, we have control of the technology to build the ships. And without the ships, no one will be able to travel into space. So yes, I believe we can control this," answers General Westbrook. "This brings us to one final point. Professor Mueller is finalizing a merger and restructuring of his company with RNR Industries. With Eric Miller and Mr. Lee's approval, I would like to have a statement of work contract in place within the next thirty days to start building a fleet of antimatter-powered spacecraft. At that time, we'll break the news to the public and go from there. Dr. Myers, I believe you have some personal business to take care of. Let me again offer my deepest condolences in the passing away of your mother. I think David Veil will be willing to give you as much time as it takes to get your affairs in order, after which it is imperative you continue to be a part of this program. Unless anyone else has something else to contribute, I think we're done here for now."

Everyone seems to take a big sigh of relief and pushes their chairs away from the table when they hear Bill Rodgers asks General Westbrook if he could clarify one point concerning hyperspeed travel, antimatter particle emissions, and healing. He wants a consensus from the group that if asked by the science community, there was no relationship between them. He briefly argues that most folks will not accept the fact that prayer healed Dr. Myers. General Westbrook takes a poll asking all those in favor of prayer to raise their hands, and everyone including but Bill Rodgers raises their hand. General Westbrook then turns to Bill Rodgers and states that he now has his answer.

Professor Mueller and George Lee talk briefly about transporting Raymond Richards and his wife out of the state. Dr. Erica Myers asks Eric Miller to follow her out into the hallway. She turns toward him and puts her hand on his arm.

"I'm so sorry I doubted you, Eric," Erica says apologetically.

"I'm not sure I would have done anything differently if I were you, Erica," admits Eric. "It took a lot of faith for you to trust me." Eric then smiles and continues, "I thank you for not putting the ether and handkerchief thing in your report."

"As far as the ether incident goes, forget it Eric, I have. And for the record," Dr. Myers continues, "there is absolutely no way I believe your engines healed my leg. With everything I have seen and heard, I believe it was prayer that healed me." Moving very close to Eric, Erica resumes; "I'd really like you to tell me more about having visions. Is there a difference between a vision and a dream?" she asks.

"Wow Erica, that's an excellent question. I think I would explain it by saying that a vision is more precise than a dream. A dream most often needs to be interpreted. When God gave me the vision of a planetary system being destroyed, I was certain it would happen exactly how I envisioned it, even though the vision did not show me a particular star. I also believe a vision can occur while we are awake, while a dream normally occurs when we are asleep."

"That makes sense to me, Eric. The first night I was at my home in Houston, I had a dream. It's amazing because I usually don't remember dreams I have, but I remember this one like I just had it, yet I can't for the life of me understand what it could mean. If I share it with you, do you think you could interpret if for me?" asks Erica.

"I'm no Daniel," admits Eric, "but I'll sure give it a shot."

"Who is Daniel?" asks Erica.

"Daniel was a prophet in the Bible known for his ability to interpret dreams," explains Eric. "So tell me, what was your dream?"

Erica starts off somewhat humorously, "Well, Daniel, I'm standing in a strange land, surrounded by people I think I know. Everyone is lost, but only I know this. I also know I'm waiting for something spectacular to happen, but for the life of me, I can't seem to focus in on it. A few seconds later, I have this premonition that the sky will open at the sound of a blast, and a blinding light will scoop me away. Suddenly, in the blink of my eye, the event comes and goes, yet I'm still there. Isn't that weird? What do you make of it? Was I having a vision about our upcoming mission?"

Eric seems stunned by what Erica has shared with him, so much to the point he takes her by the hand and leads her to some chairs further down the hallway. They sit down and Eric passionately looks at his old friend.

"What is it, Eric?" pleads Erica. "You know what this means, don't you?"

"I have a feeling what it could mean, Ricky, but I'm not sure you are going to like the answer."

Excited yet puzzled at what her long lost friend was about to reveal, Erica beckons for Eric to proceed. Deep down inside, she hopes this would be the catalyst that will solidify their relationship. Yet her heart beats strong, wondering why he thought she would not like the answer. Her fear is that he did not love her as she loved him.

Eric explains that her dream appears to represents a future event Christians refer to as the "Rapture." In this event, Jesus Christ's return represents the light who will return as close to Earth as in the clouds and in a split second take with him back to heaven those saints God gave him to save.

"But in my dream, I do not go with the light!" repeats Erica. "What happens to us? What happens to all the innocent people like myself who are left behind?"

Eric drops his head and states softly that unless they have God's spirit, they are eternally lost. He reminds Erica that he knew she would not like his answer, but also stresses that the reasons some people have dreams like this is God's way of starting to draw them into his kingdom. He senses Erica has only focused on the fact he literally told her she was not going to heaven.

With her hopes smashed that this dream was linked to a possible relationship with Eric, Erica becomes visibly upset with the fact Eric was telling her she was not going to heaven. "This is asinine. How can you say that God will not accept me into heaven, Eric Miller? I've done nothing to deserve to go to hell." Erica stands up and looks down at Eric, "I can't believe you. I've got to go back to Iowa to bury my mother, who I truly believe is in heaven right now looking down on both of us."

Erica Myers turns and starts to walk away and then sharply returns and lashes out at Eric, "But wait, you probably don't believe she is in heaven either, do you?"

Eric stands and confronts Erica, placing both his hands on her shoulders. "It's just a dream, Ricky. It doesn't have to be this way. Maybe God is trying to get your attention?"

"He has got my attention all right, mister," she shouts with a tear in her eye. "My father and mother appear to have been right about us. We could *never* be together!"

Erica Myers storms down the hallway and back into the conference room. Once there, she tracks down George, who continues to converse with Professor Mueller.

Seeing Dr. Myers approach, Professor Mueller suggests that George prepares to leave. "Call me when Mr. and Mrs. Richards are settled."

"I don't mean to interrupt you, George, but I'm ready to leave when you are," advises Dr. Myers.

Excusing himself from Professor Mueller's presence by bowing his head, George turns his attention to Dr. Myers. "I'm all set, Erica, follow me."

George and Erica exit the main office complex and walk outdoors toward one of the hangars. "How are things going with you and Eric?" asks George.

"Don't ask!" replies Erica.

"So you really don't want me to ask, or is this just your way of telling me to give you a minute and you'll explain everything?" questions George.

"And when did you become a psychologist, George?" asks Dr. Myers.

"Approximately five seconds ago, Doc!" answers George jokingly as they approach the hangar. George opens the door for Erica, and as he motions for her to enter, he notices she's been crying.

Upon entering the hangar, Erica notices a very modern and sophisticated aircraft, the only one in the huge hangar. "I'm sorry, George. But things did not go all that well between Eric and I. His religious values are difficult to understand. I'm not sure I can handle it."

"You can handle it, Erica, I know you can and will," assures George. "Eric's spiritual insight into the scriptures, as radical as they might appear, has opened many of our eyes to the knowledge of the truth." Stopping suddenly and facing Erica, George reiterates, "And we both know without his intervention, Earth might have very well been destroyed. And if we are to travel into outer space without destroying ourselves, we need to know where not to venture. We could certainly use your assistance in this area."

George and Erica enter the aircraft and find Raymond and Patricia Richards patiently resting, cuddling together on a large sofa-like chair. George walks over to Raymond and, while hugging him, lets his former employer and his wife know how pleased he is to see them. George then introduces Dr. Erica Myers, who gracefully takes a seat across from them. George takes time to explain to the Richards that Erica is going home to bury her mother before he heads to the cockpit and prepares for their departure.

Seeing the Richards cuddling together seems so incredibly natural to Dr. Erica Myers. Dr. Myers, however, cannot remember her parents ever embracing or even passionately touching. The Richards are not aware they have Erica's attention until they hear her speak to them. "Do you mind if I ask you a question?"

Looking at Erica, Pat Richards responds, "Not at all, Dr. Myers. What's on your mind?"

"I feel kind of stupid asking you this, but how do you know when you are in love? How do know when you've met the right person?" asks Erica.

Pat and Raymond look at each other before Raymond gives his wife the nod to answer the question. "That's easy," says Pat Richards. "You know you're in love when you cannot stop thinking about someone." Looking at Raymond, Pat continues, "You know he's the right one when you can't get him off you mind, or out of your system."

Raymond then adds, "It's like a chemical imbalance when you're apart from each other. Deep down inside, your body will tell you.

After a while, you'll learn to start listening to what your body is telling you. Believe me, the other person will also have a physical problem deep down in their soul and confirm your feelings. The term they use to refer to couples like this is soul mates."

Grasping her husband's hand, Pat Richards affirms, "Yes, soul mates." Slowly turning her head toward Dr. Myers, "Does that help you any, dear?"

"Absolutely," replies Erica Myers, "thank you so much for sharing that with me!" Dr. Myers then sits back into her seat, closes her eyes, and relaxes herself to sleep. Ninety minutes later, George wakes Erica informing her of their arrival in Iowa. He offers to stay with her and assist in her mother's final arrangements, but she rejects his offer. Erica hugs George and tells him she'll see him again shortly.

Eric Miller turns onto the street where Pastor Walls lives, and while his pastor's residence is three houses into the block, he notices him practicing his jumps shot. Unlike Eric's home, Pastor Walls's court is on the driveway in front of his garage, so Eric pulls into the driveway of the house just past Pastor Walls and reverses to park on the street. Pastor Walls stops playing and walks toward a slowly approaching Eric, embracing him as they hold each other more than usual. While continuing to embrace, Pastor Walls breaks the silence and whispers to Eric that he is extremely delighted to see him again. Eric releases his hold on his pastor and replies that the feeling is mutual.

Without delay, Pastor Walls jogs over to where the basketball is resting on the grass and tosses it to Eric and suggests he start the game. From the grass, Eric steps on the pavement and casually dribbles in front of a closely guarded Pastor Walls who steals the ball and drives to the hoop for an easy layup. With a lot of energy, Pastor Walls takes the ball out and with one quick step sending Eric backing up on his heels stops and sinks a ten-foot jump shot. This scene continues as Pastor Walls appears to be an NBA all-star playing against a high school freshman. Pastor Walls senses Eric Miller is playing hard but has little in the tank; nevertheless, he plays on until he wins the game.

Eric Miller shakes Pastor Walls hand and congratulates him on a game well played. Pastor Walls reaches into a cooler and retrieves two cold bottles of water, and they sit down on patio furniture behind the garage in the rear of Pastor Walls's home. Eric starts the conversation by thanking his pastor and his wife, Sandy, for their prayers. An experienced and patient Pastor Walls is silent, giving Eric time to speak in expectation he will be more forthcoming about the circumstances causing him to believe he has lied and prohibited him from confessing the last time they met.

Eric calmly continues, "I think it's time I told you exactly what I've been working on the past couple of years, Pastor. In short, I developed an engine that would propel a vehicle through space at greater than light speeds. Another engineer developed a ship that housed my engine and accompanied me on a maiden voyage into the heavens, to test our invention. That is where I have been the past two weeks. Also accompanying us on this expedition was a female doctor from the Space Agency. I left the project months ago when I thought my work was being compromised as a result of a break-in at my lab. One thing I have been holding back from you and the authorities, a lie if you will, was that I did not report anything missing due to the burglary. The truth is that some crucial components of my engines as well as the associated documents were stolen and replaced with inferior components and schematics."

Eric pauses to take a sip of water and to give Pastor Walls an opportunity to comment. Pastor Walls validates that what Eric was considering a lie was actually a withholding of the truth, to which Eric confirmed. Pastor Walls comments that what Eric considered a lie was serious but sensed there was more and gave him space to continue.

Eric resumes the conversation of the inferior components called fuel injectors by confessing to Pastor Walls that he is aware that the schematic for his superior manufactured injectors includes the ability to automatically unlock safety caps through system controls of a space vessel, but neither his injectors nor the counterfeit ones have hardware installed to satisfy this operation. Therefore, unless the safety caps are manually removed, the fuel injectors would explode and destroy the vessel. Before Pastor Walls could comment, Eric concludes that this event occurred on another vessel, and his omission of this process led to the deaths of several people. He is prepared to accept whatever disciplinary action Pastor Walls is willing to impose.

Pastor Walls asks Eric if there was anything else he wished to expound upon before he gave Eric his advice.

Eric Miller insists that he believes everything that happens is as God planned it. God ordains the beginning and the end. "God allowed me to return to the project in order to avert a catastrophic event. If it were not for the female doctor on the flight who believed in me, we might not be having this conversation. And in his infinite wisdom, God sent an old flame back into my life." Looking directly at Pastor Walls, Eric admits the female doctor who joined them on this journey, Dr. Erica Myers, was a childhood acquaintance. Some acquaintances develop into friends, and some friends become even more.

"It's weird she has a name like yours, Eric Miller, Erica Myers," observes Pastor Walls. "So where is Dr. Myers now? When are we going to meet her?"

"Well, that's a different story, Pastor," declares Eric Miller. "Dr. Myers is currently on her way to Iowa to bury her mother."

"And you're not accompanying her?"

"Right now, that's not a good idea. She left angry at me due to my interpretation of a dream she shared with me. We are both trying to come to grips with rediscovering each other," explains Eric.

Putting his arm on Eric's shoulder, Pastor Walls encourages him. "Well, my brother, if it's in God's eternal purpose that Erica is part of your life, and that your fates are tied together, then there is nothing that can destroy it. Just keep trusting in God."

"Believe me, Pastor, after having witnessed destruction everywhere, I'm well aware of God's ability to sustain us. I also paid a visit to the asteroid belt!"

In a highly excited tone, Pastor Walls turns to his friend to confirm what he just heard. "You visited the asteroid belt! Oh man, what was that like?"

"I believe with all my heart, Pastor, that the asteroid belt was once the home world of the angels, the planet Rahab. The planet God destroyed when the angels sinned."

"My God from glory, Deacon Miller, you actually did it. You actually verified what we have so often debated. The asteroid belt was a planet."

"The truth is, Pastor, from the instant God revealed this to me, I believed it. Throughout this journey, I needed to trust God, and he never let me down. I am now more than at any other time since God saved me, aware that he is in complete control of my life. I am learning to trust God without reservation and that he will send souls across my path, such as should be saved, including Dr. Erica Myers."

"If I didn't know any better, I'd say you've finally come to grips with God using you to witness to others," reflects Pastor Walls. "Or what you perceive to be the lack thereof."

"You're right, Pastor," agrees Eric. "I truly believe that God is using me in ways I might not understand or even be aware of. I would completely understand if you wanted to temporarily relieve me of my duties as a deacon." Eric finishes his water and stands up with the empty bottle. "You still recycle these?"

Standing and finishing his drink, the pastor responds, "I still got that green recycling tub in the garage." Walking in that direction, Mike continues, "There is no way I want you to lessen your duties. In fact, I want you to stand Sunday morning during altar call."

"Understood, Pastor. I think I'll go home and get some work done. Plus I need to study my lesson for tomorrow," responds Eric.

"Everything I have told you must remain between us as it's highly classified."

Pastor Walls replies, "I figured that much, my brother!"

Eric embraces his friend and brother in Christ. They pray aloud for each other, as they customarily do. They believe they'll see each other tomorrow, yet Pastor Walls watches as his friend drives out of site, as if for the last time.

Sunday morning service has started at the Grace of God Church. The choir sings the first of their two selections following the collection of the offering. Deacon Eric Miller assists in collecting the offering as he always does, taking Pastor Walls advice not to minimize his duties. After returning from the treasurer's office, Deacon Eric Miller takes his usual seat, closes his eyes, and worships God while listening to the music. The hostess on duty has entered the sanctuary and taken a seat, not expecting to greet another guest. Halfway through the choir's second selection, the door to the sanctuary opens, and a very beautiful, very well-dressed woman emerges. An usher warmly welcomes her and asks if she is a guest of a member here or just a visitor. The woman asks if Deacon Eric Miller is in attendance. The usher positively acknowledges the woman and escorts her down the main aisle. Heads turn as they pass each row of pews. The usher smiles as she stops at the pew where Deacon Eric Miller sits on the end. The usher stretches out her arm and gives the woman a program.

Sensing the usher's presence, Deacon Miller stands to let the person in. He looks long and hard at her as she gracefully moves past. Eric closes his eyes tight and searches his memory until he envisions a nameplate on a desk.

"Ms. Devereaux?" asks a puzzled Eric Miller.

She smiles, sits close to him, and softly whispers, "Yes," while reaching into her purse and handing him a card.

Eric takes the card and recognizes it as his church's welcoming card. He turns it over and notices some scriptures written on the back in his own handwriting. Baffled, he looks at her, hands the card back to her, and waits for an explanation.

"You gave this to your colleague who left it in Texas, but I believe it was truly meant for me," she whispers. "I need your help, Deacon Eric Miller. Something is happening to me, and I believe you are the key."

The choir has ended their final selection, and Pastor Walls stands in the pulpit, preparing to deliver his morning sermon. Deacon Miller opens his Bible and shares it with Elizabeth Devereaux. He does not verbally respond to her, but he lets Ms. Devereaux know he heard her, even though he does not understand the reason and nature of her request.

Pastor Walls begins his oration, "I want to thank God for being here today, for all the saints and guest in attendance, and ask that you turn your Bibles to St. John 6:44. Also turn to the book of Romans 10:13 and 14; when you have them say, amen." After hearing a few acknowledgments of amen, Elder Walls prays for today's message. "My subject this morning is 'Knowing I Am Saved,' 'Knowing I Am Saved.' Romans 10:13 states that 'for whosoever shall call upon the name of the Lord shall be saved.'

This seems rather straightforward, doesn't it? But if you continue to read on, which I always encourage the saints to do, Paul continues by asking a series of questions. 'How then shall they call on him in whom they have not believed? And how shall they believe in him of whom they have not heard? And how shall they hear without a preacher? And how shall they preach except they be sent?' What Paul is saying is that if God doesn't send a preacher to you, to preach the message God has given him, and places it in your heart to believe what his messenger has said, you *cannot* be saved. But thank God it's not up to us. St. John 6:44 reminds us that Jesus said, 'No man can come to me, except the Father which hath sent me draw him . . .' Oh saints of God, can you see it? Because it's God that has sent for you, you can be assured he will take care of you."

After hearing Pastor Walls's message to this point, Elizabeth now pleads with Eric, "What must I do to be spared?"

"Saved, Ms. Devereaux, what must you do to be saved." whispers Eric.

Elizabeth humbles herself and admits, "Forgive my ignorance in Christian terminology, Eric. I was not raised in the church."

Pastor Walls ends his sermon and begins an altar appeal. Deacon Eric Miller whispers to Elizabeth Devereaux telling her he has to go and advises her to be lead by the spirit of God as to what to do next.

Deacon Eric Miller takes a position in the front of the church on the same side as he was sitting, extends his hands, and starts to browse the audience. Sandy Walls takes a position in front of the opposite side of the aisle. Elizabeth Devereaux instantly recognizes this scene as the one in her dream. Deacon Eric Miller looks in her direction and stretches out his hand to her. A nervous Elizabeth Devereaux rises from her seat and starts to walk toward Deacon Eric Miller, who meets her half way up the aisle. As soon as he grabs her hand, Elizabeth starts to chant those unrecognizable words she had recorded in her father's home. Sandy Walls comes over to assist Deacon Eric Miller and asks Elizabeth Devereaux why she approached the altar, who in tears between the foreign speech manages to tell Sandy Walls she wants to be saved. They escort Elizabeth to a dressing room behind the pulpit.

Once inside the dressing room, the three sit down in a circle, and Eric introduces his guest to Sandy. "Ms. Devereaux, this is Evangelist Sandy Walls, Pastor Walls's wife. We are both altar workers here at our church." Turning his attention to Evangelist Sandy Walls, Deacon Miller continues, "Evangelist Walls, this is Ms. Elizabeth Devereaux. I met Ms. Devereaux at the Space Agency in Houston, where the last I knew, she was a receptionist." Taking a deep breath, Eric returns his attention to his guest. "Now tell me, Ms. Devereaux, what brings you to Michigan? What is going on?"

A much more relaxed Ms. Devereaux begins, "First of all, please call me Elizabeth. Well, I guess it started a couple of weeks ago. I came to Michigan because my father was critically injured in a car accident that he did not survive. There was a memorial, I buried him, and after a gathering at his home, I fell asleep and had a dream. In that dream, many people were standing around waiting for some light from heaven to take them away. A man in a church was standing in the front of a church with his hands extended, while another man was petitioning to folks to come forward. When I woke up from the dream, I found myself mumbling uncontrollably." Elizabeth produces a small tape recorder from her purse and presses play. Deacon Miller and Evangelist Walls listen.

"She is speaking in tongues," says Evangelist Walls. "The Holy Ghost is manifesting itself in her. You have the Holy Ghost, my dear."

"I don't know what that is or what it means," admits Elizabeth. "All I know is that afterward, I sought to find the man from my dream. It took a few days, but I finally recognized the man in the building. It was you, Eric Miller."

"That's amazing Elizabeth," admits Deacon Miller. "So tell Evangelist Walls how you found me."

"I was fumbling around in my purse, I believe dealing with the tape recorder, when I came across a church welcoming card you left for your partner when you visited the agency a few weeks ago. The card has this address on it."

"Wow! That can only be God. That can only be the working of the Holy Ghost," describes Evangelist Walls. "Elizabeth, God has given you his spirit. The only thing left is for us to baptize you in Jesus's name. This is done to publicly identify you with the man who has died for the sin you are charged with, the original sin of Adam. Are you ready, my dear?"

"I guess," says Elizabeth. "Can you explain what is happening to me?"

"Of course, dear," explains Evangelist Walls. "Almighty God has called you, chosen you to be in his kingdom and given you his spirit as a sign unto you. This is evident to us by you speaking in an unknown language. We sometimes call it speaking in tongues. This is all finalized by a ceremonial ritual called baptism. This publicly identifies you with the man who made this all possible, God's son, Jesus Christ, whose name will be called over you in baptism."

Evangelist Walls motions for Deacon Miller to prepare himself for baptizing Elizabeth and to inform her husband Pastor Walls. She then assists Elizabeth in changing her clothes. While Elizabeth is undressing, she asks Evangelist Walls, "What is the significance of my dream?"

Sandy picks up her Bible, turns to 1 Thessalonians 4, and begins reading at verse 13, "For I would not have you ignorant, brethren, concerning them which are asleep, that ye sorrow not, even as others which have no hope. For if we believe that Jesus Christ died and rose again, even so them also which sleep in Jesus Christ (or saints that have died) will God bring with him. For this we say unto you by the word of the Lord, that we which are alive and remain unto the coming of the Lord shall not prevent them which are asleep. For the Lord himself shall descend from heaven with a shout, with the voice of the archangel, and with the trump of God: and the dead in Christ shall rise first. Now this is where I assume your dream comes in, Elizabeth. Then we which are alive and remain shall be caught up together with them in the clouds, to meet the Lord in the air: and so shall we ever be with the Lord. Your dream was of an event we call the Rapture."

Having changed out of her clothes and into a baptismal gown, Elizabeth comments, "I believe what you are telling me, Evangelist Walls, but I can't say I understand."

"In time, God will open up your understanding, but the primary thing is belief of the truth. God has given you this too, and you should be thankful. Not everyone will have this opportunity," confesses Evangelist Walls. "The scripture in Matthew 22:14 says that many are called, but few are chosen. Are you ready?"

"Yes, ma'am, I'm ready," says Elizabeth, shivering in her baptismal clothing. "I'm a little chilly, but I'm ready. What should I expect?"

Evangelist Walls wraps a blanket around Elizabeth, embraces her, and prays with her. When she finishes her prayer, Sandy explains, "Expect when you come out of the water to be changed. Just remember to praise God for what he has already done for you."

The two women leave the dressing room and walk up the stairs to a large tub of water where Deacon Eric Miller is waiting. Evangelist Walls assists Ms. Devereaux down some stairs to meet Eric, who takes her by the hand and slowly proceeds to the center of the pool. Deacon Miller instructs Elizabeth as to how he must totally submerge her under water but will bring her back up quickly. He also encourages her as Evangelist Walls has done to praise God for what he has done for her. Elizabeth is not really sure what they mean but accepts their advice. She hears many people around praying and chanting but can't see them. All becomes quiet as she hears Pastor Walls say a prayer, followed by Deacon Eric Miller's prayer, but only remembers hearing him say "in Jesus's name" before she is plunged into the water. Seconds later, she is lifted up and while trying to say thank you, God, hears herself uttering words she did not know and unable to stop. She is vaguely aware of people cheering and clapping while Evangelist Walls is helping her out of the pool. She also feels very warm as if she has been smothered in warm oil. The next few minutes are lost to her. When she finally comes to her senses, she is sitting in the main sanctuary, fully dressed with Evangelist Walls, Pastor Walls, and Deacon Miller. The rest of the church is empty.

"What, what's going on?" asks Elizabeth. "I feel as if I'm returning from another world."

Sandy giggles, "Interesting choice of words, my dear. The way you've been praising God for the last forty-five minutes, I'd sure say you've been in another world."

"I feel great. I feel warm. Is it a little hot in here?" asks Elizabeth.

"One thing you need to know, Elizabeth, is that that warm feeling could be categorized as being sealed by God and a new creature in Christ Jesus," explains Pastor Walls. "Every born-again Christian experiences some kind of metamorphosis associated with their conversion and new birth experience."

"So this feeling will last forever?" asks Elizabeth.

Deacon Eric Miller continues, "You have the gift of God. You have eternal life, Sister Devereaux. And eternal life is just as it says. It's eternal. It will last forever."

An inquisitive Elizabeth continues her barrage of questions, "So what is my fate? What is my destiny?"

"Naturally, ones fate and ones destiny is a mystery, until we pass through history," explains Deacon Eric Miller. "Spiritually, our destiny is to be conformed to the image of God's son. However, a man's ultimate fate lies in where God puts him in eternity!"

Elizabeth Devereaux takes a deep breath. "So what's next?"

ONLY GOD KNOWS

I n the months to come, Elizabeth Devereaux totally moves to Michigan, is literally adopted by Pastor and Evangelist Walls, becomes a faithful member of Grace of God Church, and begins working on her law degree. She is also employed as a receptionist at the new RNR Industries. Only God knows what else is in her future.

Professor Mueller is now the president of a new RNR Industries that includes an engineering division that absorbed his former company Mueller Engineering and Eric Miller's EM Laboratories division, which designs engines.

George Lee is a vice president of RNR Industries, which has a contract to manufacture spacecraft for the government. He and Eric Miller also formed a school training troubled teens and gang members in hyperspace fuel systems and piloting. They are extremely concerned as to where God will lead this generation of engineers. However, within weeks after starting the formation of the new RNR Industries, Eric Miller pilots the *Argo Navis* back to the asteroid belt and builds another laboratory. He teaches his students from that laboratory.

Bill Rodgers and David Veil are working on building an outpost to monitor activity in the forbidden region of space and to collect data on its delicate properties. Their goal is to disprove any theories that this region of space has human tissue regenerative powers.

Dr. Erica Myers eventually moves to an office complex on the campus of RNR Industries as a liaison for the Space Agency, reporting directly to General Westbrook. Dr. Erica Myers and Eric Miller have not spoken to each other since their conversation after the mission briefing, but they think of each other daily.

Only God knows the whereabouts of Pat and Raymond Richards. And only God knows what will happen next to Eric Miller and Dr. Erica Myers.

If you want to know, you'll have to read the second half of this amazing story entitled *Destruction of Disbelief*, Available at http://Trafford.com.